I0519517

DARKNESS IN THE STAR CHAMBER
© 2016 Robert Storey White

Edited by
Shirley Reusch

Illustrated by
Faith Parenti

First Edition
2016

Published by
Thesis Antithesis Synthesis Press
2016
at

www.thesis-antithesis-synthesis.com

I thank the lovely Ms. Faith Parenti for encouraging me to write a piece of historical fiction, not limited by facts, which is truer than anything that really happened.

This book is dedicated to abolishing the business of bankruptcy.

About this Book

"**Darkness In The Star Chamber**" is historical fiction. It takes place where bankruptcies began when the Realm was dominated by a merciless Warlord who reached "Arrangements" with Citizens taking everything they owned in exchange for relieving their debts after giving their property to the Warlord's Club of Members. The People revolted against this greedy Master after all the wealth in the Kingdom was in the hands of the Master and his clandestine syndicate of co-conspirators.

About the Author

Robert White was born in Annapolis Maryland on October 25, 1949. Robert's Mother was a school teacher and his Father was a career Navy aircraft mechanic who served in the South Pacific during WWII. Robert grew up in Panama, South Texas, and Southern California. He played high school and college football and later returned to Cimarron County Oklahoma in the 70's to rebuild his Great Grandparents homestead on the Cimarron River. Robert co- developed the FastSURF and FastSOLID surface and solid modeling software in the 90's and sold those products to the company declaring bankruptcy discussed in his other book on bankruptcy - "**Canary In The Court**". Robert has four adult Children and five Grand Children. Robert was previously married and is presently in a 21 year relationship with the lovely Ms. Faith Parenti and is looking forward to marrying once again.

Table of Contents

Prologue

My first book about bankruptcy, "**Canary In The Court**", was limited to what really occurred in the case chronicled in that book. As mom said "It might not be right but it's true" and "**Canary In The Court**" is certainly true. "**Darkness In The Star Chamber**" on the other hand is not constrained by facts yet it is true nonetheless. "**Darkness In The Star Chamber**" is historical fiction depicting the origins of the mess we call bankruptcy.

Bankruptcy turns normal rules of commercial enterprise upside down. Bankruptcy rewards the debtor's failures at the expense of creditors' successes. Bankruptcy is a federally subsidized insurance policy protecting risk takers from their poor choices. It is a publically financed Casino redistributing wealth. In Bankruptcy Court contracts are broken, debt is discharged, and the debtor's property is sold for less than value to buyers who escape liability while creditors go unpaid. Bankruptcy Courts compete for business by offering the best deals to debtors in exchange for their patronage. Lawyers from local "Bankruptcy Rings" control the practice of law in their regions. Attorneys gorge on estate funds depleting the dividend intended for creditors. This is not the Congressional intent of the Bankruptcy Code but it has become the practice.

Bankruptcy Courts have extended their jurisdiction beyond limit into every aspect of law including incarcerating parties within the Court's reach. Bankruptcy Law has replaced the US Constitution in regulating commercial enterprise. Rights once protected by the Constitution are routinely violated by the bankruptcy bench and bar.

If this trend is not reversed our economy will continue to decline from exploitation by the clandestine syndicate of co-conspirators practicing bankruptcy. If this exploitation is not stopped we are doomed to repeat the horrors of "Darkness In The Star Chamber".

DARKNESS IN THE STAR CHAMBER

The Outer Chamber

Members of the Court enter the Outer Chamber dressed in woolen suits of contemporary style. Their polished leather shoes and belts accentuate the dress code. Many wear hats denoting their status in this pre-secular society. The Outer Chamber shows no sign of the struggles within. The granite floor is worn smooth by foot traffic. The official flag and seal appoint the wood-clad walls inviting a false sense of dignity.

Members are feudally loyal to the Court in exchange for privileges bequeathed to them. Members respectfully argue but are not allowed to win. Rights claimed here are contrived by Man, not granted by God. These rights are quite alienable. Interpretation changes daily and violations are common.

Citizens with requests of the Court are ushered into the Outer Chamber and represented by a Member. Members bicker in dispute but the outcome is not theirs. Decisions belong to chance. Arbitrariness insures that unpredictability reenforces obedience.

Most Citizens appearing here can not afford to pay their debts and seek forgiveness from the Court. The appointed Member negotiates an Arrangement between the Citizen and the Court. Arrangements require that Citizens surrender all assets to the Court in exchange for relief. Creditors who demand repayment are led to another chamber with a clear and convincing view of the dungeon. Arrangements are never opposed except by Members graveling over a bigger share. Once an Arrangement is reached the Citizen is led into the Star Chamber to agree or consider other options. Other options include prison, brutality, or banishment from the Realm.

The Star Chamber

The Star Chamber is concealed within the Outer Chamber. The Star Chamber has a spirit all its own as if resident evil occupies the room. The Star Chamber is not to be understood it is simply to be feared. Enter the Star Chamber and you enter the world of deceit, greed, and corruption. Enter without pre-arranged forgiveness and brutality is your fate.

A hooded Guard stands at the door to enforce order. He displays a weapon dangling from his waistband. For close encounters he hides a thin blade in his boot. He is a farmer by birthright and practices his weaponry by slaughtering his dinner.

"All rise and draw near," the Guard beckons with a cruel smirk under his hood.

An ominous hush overtakes the Star Chamber before business begins. The Room sighs in a long breath as Members prepare for battle.

A pale Scribe sits by the side recording the transfer of assets.

"Scratch, dash, click," he inscribes upon the parchment record.

Then the Master enters the Star Chamber and takes his place at the Dias. Members jump to attention. Their collective rustling sounds like a band of thieves falling through the gallows.

"Scoot, rise, scoot," echos their shuffling in unison.

The Master nods and Members slowly relax at ease. They quietly sink back into submission showing well practiced respect. Not another word, not another sound, not another move had better draw attention to their presence. Not yet.

The Master unpacks his satchel placing its contents on the elevated Dias for all to see. A bronze scale, wood gavel, and ordinary feather decorate the alter of law. The Master places the feather on one tray and the gavel on the other tipping the scale permanently out of balance. "Guilty until proven innocent" is his motto. "Don't ask" is his message.

Members swallow hard with anxiety. Lose too many cases and they might be demoted to the Class of ordinary Citizen. Taunt throats strain to quiet voices deep within.

"Run fool," one throat growls.

"You're next," another groans.

"He's a monster," the unspoken truth squeaks out.

Throats clear again to complete the ritual before Court begins.

"The Court's coffers dwindle from excessive withdrawals," the Master complains.

"Who here has a remedy to reverse this disgrace?" the Master offers opportunity to any enterprising Member.

Heads dart side to side as Members search for the next volunteer. The first to sacrifice their client may win favor with the Master but will certainly lose payment for their services.

The newest Member rises proudly and awaits recognition.

"Y-e-s," the Master acknowledges with drawn out intent.

"My client is prepared to surrender all worldly possessions in exchange for relief from his debts," the novice offers.

"They are ALL willing to surrender unto me!" the Master rebuts.

"Is there m-o-r-e?" lay his question.

"My client is prepared to make a substantial contribution to the Court," the aspiring Member informs.

"How substantial?" inquires the greedy Master.

"One hundred coin," the self-promoting Member boasts.

"Step forward," the Master commands.

The Guard quickly intercepts the naive Member, rudely

bumping him off stride. The Guard hands the Member a black cloth bag with a gilded drawstring.

> "Take your client into a sidebar and return with his offering," orders the Master.

> "Done," promises the faithful Member seeking higher rank.

The Master rules by force, not authority. Authority will come a century later from the word of God appointing a future Master as King. For now Citizens rally around the strongest Warlord who protects them from foreign invaders. Flaming airborne missiles raining death from above await Citizens either way.

The Origin of Power

Punishment, obedience, and loyalty are the same. They are the price paid to reside in the Master's Realm. Punishment promotes obedience which instills loyalty. Loyalty preserves harmony which guarantees domestic tranquility. Disobedience is the coward's choice because the loyal punish themselves.

Terror is the Master's kindest punishment because fear unites quicker than anger. Fear spreads hysterically throughout the Realm whereas anger rests with the individual. Threaten a man's family not himself. Convert his property not his beliefs. A man fears for his family and property and is only angered by threats against his body and beliefs. The Master struggles to appreciate these rules.

The Master was once the Realm's fiercest Warlord before he abdicated his command so he could preside over the Court. The Court can extract more payment from Citizens than the army. An army at war with its own Citizens has an equal for an enemy. Citizens have short supply lines and superior knowledge of the local terrain. An army fighting its Citizens risks overthrow from within whereas a Court punishing its Citizens attracts approval from the crowd.

The Master longs to be an artist. His mother came from an alien people with different beliefs. He fears discovery as a homosexual so he took a bride who he convinced to commit suicide. Anguish erupts from his psyche in the form of violence against all people. He has discovered the secret of power.

At night the Master broods over respect. He lays awake in a sleepless dream punishing those at his mercy. The dream repeats like a hallucinogenic fever. Were he less compulsive the Master could free himself from this reoccurring trap but his fascination with power makes him addicted to thoughts of punishment.

The Master leads by fear not by example. Restraint does not caution his brutality. Members eager to please reinforce his cruelty. Precedent is his to give and take. When power is taken monestrous men rule but when power is given the timid govern.

The Citizen's Gambit

The Citizen enters the Star Chamber eager to learn his Arrangement. He believes he knows the rules. Surrender all possessions and all debt will be forgiven. He has offered one hundred coin to the Court as payment for relief from his debts.

"Do you understand the Arrangement?" barks the Master.

"Yes," is the only answer allowed.

"And why do you offer this one hundred coin?" begins the inquisition.

"Out of respect," the Citizen replies as taught by his Representative.

"Have you no more coin?" the Master reveals his thieving motives.

"Yes, but I need it for food and clothing," claims the Citizen.

"Grow your own food and make your own cloths!" the Master commands angrily.

"Yes Master," capitulates the Citizen.

"Or maybe you will offer your daughter as settlement?" insinuates the Master.

"Please, take the rest of my coin," the Citizen mistakenly tries to negotiate.

"Is she a fair maiden?" the Master imagines.

"Very fair I am sure," the proud father defends.

"Bring her to me!" roars the Master.

"Please Sire, you can have all my coin," the Citizen begs in despair.

"I'll have your coin and daughter," the Master expands the bargain.

"I'd rather you take my life," the Citizen counters the ultimatum.

How quickly negotiations in the Star Chamber resort to life or death. The Master knows he must take the coin, leave the daughter, and spare the Citizen's life else the dead man takes his hidden treasure to the grave.

The Master has played this game before and knows his nemesis in the Star Chamber are the Members not Citizens. Members must be taught to remain silent and not betray the exploitation. Rewards for loyalty must be handed out in equal measure with punishment.

"Who among you has a solution?" invites the Master.

The Member representing the Citizen knows it is not his place to speak. Older Members know the first to speak will escape punishment by playing the game.

"Spare the daughter and hang the Citizen," spoke the wiser of Members, reminding the Court that the Citizen offered his own life in exchange for his daughter's.

"Torture the Citizen and you can have both his daughter and coin," ventured another Member who had not thought things through; although the terror perceived in this recommendation garnered the Master's approval.

"Take the coin and spare both the daughter and the Citizen," another Member suggested, putting the bargaining back where it began.

All heads turned toward this last suggestion knowing it angered the Master because it relieved the most amount of fear. The Master nodded to the Guard who seized the Member and led him away never to be seen again. Members were expendable if they could not help maintain terror in the Star Chamber.

"Keep your daughter's chaste and bring me the rest of your coin," the Master directed, disregarding all appearance of impropriety.

The Distribution

After the Citizen surrendered all his coin and his Representative converted the rest of his property to more coin the Arrangement was ready to be distributed in tribute. Half went to the Master to maintain the Realm. One quarter was reserved for the Citizen's Representative. The remainder was distributed to the syndicate of Members perpetrating the fraud.

This illicit Cabal of co-conspirators practicing Arrangements operated with immunity as long as they brought coin into the Court. They controlled access to the Court and colluded with the Master to fleece the honest but unfortunate Citizen. Creditors demanding that debts be repaid were jailed. Creditors cooperating with the Court were repaid just enough to lend to another Citizen to perpetuate the cycle of debt and Arrangements.

The enterprise of Arrangements was born in secrecy. The rules and precedents changed frequently but the final outcome was always the same. Each Citizen was stripped of their property which was then redistributed among the syndicate.

Creditors turned a blind eye in exchange for a few ounces of flesh carved off the dying carcass. Arrangements thus became the first criminal conspiracy in history authorized by the Court.

The Court flourished under this regime. The Treasury overflowed even though accountings became less precise. Coin disappeared when exchanged between Members. More and more Arrangements were negotiated but the economy grew weaker and weaker. The ideology of Arrangements was profitable for the Realm but only made more Arrangements necessary for Citizens.

Geoff's Machine

Geoff was a Blacksmith. He invented a self-propelled irrigation motor at a time when farmers carried water in buckets to irrigate their fields. His invention combined a waterwheel with an Archimedes screw. He didn't invent the waterwheel or Archimedes screw but simply connected them to create a motor that lifted water out of the stream and onto the field.

The genius of his invention was hidden within a sealed box linking the wheel to the screw. Inside the metal box were two bronze gears driven by the rotation of the waterwheel which in turn rotated the Archimedes screw, which lifted the water onto the field. The box hiding the gears was sealed by rivets fusing its metal sides together. The secrets within would be destroyed if the box were forcibly opened.

Geoff's invention doubled crop production and with less labor. Geoff sold every irrigation motor he could build. To protect his invention he had to work in secrecy and could not risk hiring help who might steal his design.

His success was also his failure. With more and more orders he purchased more and more materials but could not keep up with delivering motors. His bills went unpaid and eventually he too needed an Arrangement.

A traveling Merchant from the Orient was touring the Realm selling silk, spice, and ladanum . The Merchant was a spy using his wears as a cover to make an introduction. Once having made your acquaintance the Merchant took note of your methods and practices. The Merchant had never seen a self-propelled irrigation motor so he offered to purchase Geoff's design. Being in debt Geoff considered the Merchant's proposal.

The Merchant could not afford to purchase Geoff's invention outright so he promised to pay Geoff a percent of every motor the Merchant could sell. The Merchant had enough money to pay Geoff's creditors to get him out of debt if Geoff would continue building motors for the Merchant. The Merchant would then become Geoff's silent partner.

A deal was struck and Geoff's invention now belonged to the Merchant, but the motor's design was known only by Geoff. Geoff worked hard but slipped back into debt. The same cycle of missed deliveries and unpaid bills plagued Geoff. Soon Geoff's creditors forced him into an Arrangement.

Geoff considered hiring a Member as a Representative but the Merchant claimed he understood the law of Arrangements. The Merchant appeared before the Court once Geoff was summonsed.

"Where is the Blacksmith?" challenged the Master not recognizing the Merchant.

"If I may speak I wish to serve as Representative," informed the Merchant.

"Do I know you?" doubted the Master.

"No Sire, but I travel the world and am familiar with laws of trade," the Merchant began weaving his own noose.

"What interest do you have in this Arrangement?" demanded the Master.

"I own the Blacksmith's only means of support," the Merchant informed the Court.

"Can the Blacksmith dig wells?" proposed the Master.

"I imagine he can," surmised the Merchant.

"Then he can support himself," concluded the Master.

"I meant to say I own the Blacksmith's only property," the Merchant corrected.

"The Court owns all of the Blacksmith's property now," the Master countered.

"But we shook hands my Master," the Merchant tried to argue.

"I'll shake your head and you'll own nothing," the Master threatened.

"We had an agreement," the Merchant defended.

"And I have an Arrangement," the Master warned.

"Very well," the Merchant surrendered.

"And what property belonging to the Arrangement do you claim to own?" the Master started gathering facts.

"I purchased rights to the Blacksmith's invention," the Merchant confessed.

"And what is this invention?" the curious Master wanted to know.

"A self-propelled irrigation motor," the Merchant disclosed.

"How is this machine constructed?" the Master assessed.

"Only the Blacksmith knows," the Merchant alleged.

"So you claim to own his mind?" the Master deduced.

"It might be said so," the Merchant agreed.

"I own the minds of my Subjects," the Master proclaimed.

"I see the problem," the Merchant reconciled.

"Will you deliver his mind or his property?" the Master pressed on.

"I own neither," the Merchant conceded.

"But that creates a bigger problem," the Master explained.

"If you own neither the Blacksmith's mind nor his invention but he thinks you do then he will not surrender his design to the Court," the Master revealed the paradox.

"Secrets and hidden coins are difficult to uncover through force," the Master shared.

"What do you propose Master?" the Merchant engaged.

"Steal his design and bring it to the Court," the Master revealed.

"And return with an expert to explain the workings of the machine," the Master recommended.

"May that expert be the Blacksmith himself?" the Merchant tried to simplify.

"I would think not," the Master concluded.

"May that expert be me?" the Merchant anticipated his dilemma.

"If you return knowing the secrets of the design," the Master allowed.

Work All Night

The Merchant grabbed Geoff on the way out of Court.

"What is the Arrangement?" Geoff inquired.

"To provide a machine," disclosed the Merchant.

"But none are built," panicked Geoff.

"Then we must work all night and build one," the Merchant demanded.

"You did not pay to know my design," Geoff complained.

"The Court will know your mind soon enough," the Merchant warned.

Geoff and the Merchant hurried to the shop. Parts for the machine were scattered all about. Geoff gathered enough pieces to assemble a whole motor. The men donned gloves and aprons. Geoff fired the forge and organized his tools. His first task was to hammer the Archimedes screw into shape. This was no secret someone could not already see.

"How can I help?" offered the Merchant.

"Can you work with wood?" asked Geoff.

"I build furniture at home," revealed the Merchant.

"Then you can assemble the waterwheel," Geoff permitted.

The two men worked to exhaustion well into the night. Geoff checked the Merchant's progress which was finally complete. Geoff was ready to join the water wheel to the Archimedes screw by the secrets within the box.

"The next step is tricky," Geoff warned.

Geoff slipped a plate with a large hole over the shaft of the waterwheel and attached a washer, bushing, gear, and pin. He did the same for the Archimedes Screw. Then he connected the shafts and gears by joining the other sides of the box, drawing the gears into contact. He hammered one rivet into each edge of the plates forming the box, fusing the housing into a rigid structure.

"I must rest," Geoff requested.

"I'll finish at sunrise," he planned.

The Merchant reached into his chest of silk and spice and withdrew an vile of ladanum.

"This will make your sleep short but sweet," the Merchant assured.

"What is it?" Geoff asked.

"Dreams of Angels," fancied the Merchant.

Geoff swallowed the potion and collapsed into his chair. His eyes flickered open and shut. Smoke from the forge swirled upward into the shape of a Vixen. She motioned for Geoff's embrace and enveloped him like a warm bath. He succumbed to her affection, returning kisses into the air. He knew her as the Angel of Sleep.

The Merchant took a different potion. It was the Devil's Spice denying sleep for days. Instead of Angels the Merchant saw gargoyles and beasts. He completed the box by stuffing wooden dowels into the holes made to receive the remaining rivets. He rolled the machine off the bench into a wheelbarrow and loaded it in the cart outside. The Merchant's strength doubled with each taste of Devil's Spice.

The Merchant pushed the cart all the way to town by himself, arriving after sun up. At the courthouse steps he summonsed the Guard to help hoist the machine into the Star Chamber. The Guard called the Court into emergency session. No other parties appeared before the Master.

"Is this the machine?" quarried the Master.

"Indeed it is," replied the Merchant in pride.

"How does it work?" the Master pried further.

"By the gears in this sealed box," revealed the Merchant.

"Show them to me," the Master instructed.

The Merchant withdrew the lose wooden dowels from the plates forming the box. He rotated the plates around the metal rivets remaining in the edges holding the box together. Within the exposed box were two gears meshing to form a drive. No one had ever seen such a mechanism before. The Master studied the design trying to commit its secrets to memory.

"How do you make the gears?" was the Master's ultimate question.

"I am not skilled in such things," the Merchant confessed.

"I could carve them from wood but not from bronze," the Merchant conceded.

"Who knows this form of metalworking?" the Master wanted to know.

"These methods are new to your Realm," the Merchant informed.

"Then we must create an Arrangement requiring the Blacksmith to work for the Court," realized the Master.

"What will be my compensation for securing the Blacksmith's employment?" ventured the Merchant.

"Your freedom," leveraged the Master.

Partner Employer Swindler

The Merchant returned to Geoff's shop to awaken the Blacksmith.

"What time is it?" Geoff wondered.

"Noon," the Merchant revealed, realizing Geoff would be alarmed.

"We're late. We must hurry!" Geoff tried to move.

"I appeared for you," the Merchant informed.

"Where is the motor?" Geoff asked in distress.

"I took it to Court to secure your bail," the Merchant misrepresented.

"Am I under arrest?" Geoff panicked.

"You would have been," the Merchant assured.

"What is the Arrangement?" Geoff inquired as to his rights and responsibilities.

"To build more motors," the Merchant asserted.

"Do we have orders?" Geoff anticipated.

"Yes, Orders from the Court", the Merchant emphasized.

A pause slowed their discourse. Each man reevaluated his liabilities. Geoff was in the dark as to the Arrangement but enlightened as to his invention. Only he knew how to construct the machine. Seeing the inner working of his mechanism was not the same as knowing how to build it.

The Merchant on the other hand had more ladanum and planned to use it. He knew the first Angel to visit Geoff was a Vixen not a Saint. The Merchant knew Geoff was vulnerable. Few mortals can resist temptation from an ethereal Vixen. The Vixen was an illusion not subject to rejection.

"What was that potion you gave me last night?" Geoff remembered.

"Did you sleep?" deflected the Merchant.

"I over slept," Geoff admitted.

"When you are worried the potion sometimes works that way," the Merchant apologized.

"Who was that woman you brought to me?" Geoff pretended not to know.

"The potion brings what you need," the Merchant explained.

"I need an Arrangement so I can have a real woman," Geoff objected.

"A real woman might be beyond imagination," the Merchant advised from experience.

"What does that mean?" Geoff felt he was being mocked.

"It means that more potion will bring the truth", the Merchant offered in distraction.

Geoff took more laudanum and relaxed in a wide awake vision. The Vixen appeared again but rebuffed his affection. She seemed more attracted to the Merchant than Geoff. Geoff's anger confused his perception. He felt worthless with self pity which made him aggressive. Geoff rose against the Merchant ready to do violence.

"You've taken my woman," Geoff accused the Merchant.

The alarmed Merchant realized Geoff confused the Vixen for Geoff's lost invention. The Merchant had seen such spells overcome creative men. Imagination was both a gift and curse. Without discipline imagination becomes delusional. The Merchant must redirect Geoff's hallucinating genius.

"She is yours, I do not know her," the Merchant tried to claim.

"You know her, you stole her from me," Geoff was

certain.

"I offered her to you in exchange for your freedom," the Merchant corrected.

"She IS my freedom?" Geoff became confused by his own words.

"Our bargain was for your machine not the Vixen," the Merchant tried to break the spell.

Geoff slowly became aware he was dwelling to two worlds at once. Words from one world explained visions from the other. His vision and invention melded into one illusion. He realized how easily his mind could be turned against him. Everything happened so fast. Debt, his bargain with the Merchant, and the Arrangement all speed by in a blur. There was no time to think. He must change the equation of time or lose his mind.

The Merchant had to salvage the situation. A bargain is a bargain he tried to explain. A man's handshake is his word even though the Merchant's loyalty was secretly pledged to the Court. The concept of two Masters was not in conflict anyway because it made no sense to begin with. The Master was the only Ruler and Geoff's was his Subject.

"You need to teach me the secret of your design," the Merchant asserted.

"In exchange for what?" Geoff resisted.

"Your life you fool!" the Merchant leveled.

"Your life you fool!", Geoff accused back.

"But I am free to travel the Realm," the Merchant exposed his getaway plan.

"You on the other hand are confined to this shop," the Merchant assured.

"I can not teach you all the secrets of my design," Geoff disclosed.

"Why not?" the Merchant demanded.

"They are known by others, not me," Geoff confessed.

The Merchant began to fear the limits of his bargain. The Merchant always suspected Geoff was not the designer of his machine. The Merchant had not actually purchased Geoff's design because Geoff did not own it.

"Who knows all the secrets of the design?" the Merchant exposed his plot.

"The Miner, the Mathematician, the Sculptor, and the Potter," Geoff revealed.

"How are they involved?" the Merchant demanded to know.

"The Miner finds the ore and I smelt it.   The Mathematician calculates the angles on the gears and the Sculptor carves them.   Then the Potter forms the mold," Geoff revealed the complex process.

"What do you do?" the Merchant stood confused.

"I hammer the iron into shape and pour bronze into the mold to form the gears," Geoff revealed the process.

"Who builds the waterwheel?" the Merchant inquired further.

"You do!" Geoff retorted.

The Merchant went from partner to employer to swindler with Geoff's complete disclosure.   The Merchant invested in a man who owned nothing and then bought what that man did not own.   To add insult to injury the Merchant told the Court he employed Geoff and would swindle him out his invention, which now would be impossible.

Precedent

The day of reckoning was at hand. The Merchant was to appear before the Court to explain the secrets of Geoff's invention. The Merchant tried to enter the Star Chamber but the Guard would not let him pass.

"Of course," the Merchant realized.

"I am not allowed to enter until summonsed," the Merchant conceded.

"I'll wait in the Outer Chamber until called," the Merchant agreed as directed.

Members of the Court filed by the Merchant on their way into the Star Chamber, gazing upon him like a tortured spectacle. They were sure new law was about to be written and it never happened peacefully.

Members took their seats row by row in front of the Dias. The Master entered the Star Chamber dressed in his most formal regalia. He wore a satin robe with gilded collar and a silk fez embroidered with the Realm's emblem. He carried a staff topped with a cloudy crystalline orb. All the Master's accouterments announced this was to be a day of precedent. Without command Members rose and waited for the Master to be seated. Normal etiquette would not satisfy today's solemn occasion. Members remained standing until directed by the Master.

"Summons the Merchant,"the Master ordered the Guard.

The Merchant entered the Star Chamber with all eyes upon him. The Merchant was versed in diplomacy and recognized an ambush when he saw one. The Merchant was also skilled at wagering and knew the game was not lost until the last card was played.

The Master nodded and all were seated. The Guard drew near as a threat against dissent. No artifacts decorated the Dias this day except the mysterious orb atop the staff appearing to hover weightless on its own.

"Have you discovered the secret of the machine?" the Master cut to the chase.

"Yes Sire, but there are only more secrets," the Merchant lamented.

Members groaned as if they were the victim of this inquest. Members were learned men but not intelligent. They had stuffed their heads with facts and law but could not make sense of either until told. They often confused cause with effect, juxtaposing time, rearranging the past with the future, twisting logic into a convenience - not the truth. When the future determines the past then precedent determines itself.

"What secrets, how many, who knows them?" the Master was losing patience.

"The design is more complex than I was aware of. The Blacksmith contracts with others to supply parts for the machine," the Merchant was sure the Master did not want to hear.

"Bring them all to me," the Master ordered before he considered the limits of his power.

A moan reverberated amongst Members. The dirty little secret exposing the Master's limited power over parties not privy to the Arrangement was about to be tested. It was not that the Master's power was limited for it clearly was not. The Master's power was absolute. However that power had never been tested to take control over others not part of the Arrangement. While absolute power needs no excuse taking jurisdiction over strangers to the Arrangement does.

The Member in charge of liquidating the Arrangement stood to address the Court.

"May I inquire if the secrets are known by other tradesmen?" the Member contemplated.

"Some tradesmen, some laymen, some scholars," the Merchant disclosed.

"Scholars," the murmur rose to an audible concern.

"What kind of scholars?" the Master hesitated to know.

"A Mathematician," the Merchant reluctantly disclosed.

The murmur returned to a groan. Only a Physician's prescription trumped the power of the Court because the sick can not be made to appear. But a Mathematician's intellect trumped not only the power of the Court but the law itself. A Mathematician's Law was invariant, not arbitrary, or subject to fickle translation like the Court's law. Few Members knew the language of Math. Mathematicians counted with letters and symbols, not numbers. Goat herders and Members counted with numbers. And chances were the Mathematician was also designing weapons for the Realm - not an easy person to jail. The Master's limit of power was due to his limited knowledge.

The Master sighed deeply and turned away from Members so as not to appear concerned. He stared into the mysterious orb looking for his next inspiration. How could the Blacksmith's agreements with other tradesmen be made property of the Court?

"Does the Blacksmith have contracts for the delivery of materials?" the Master began his groundwork.

"Yes - payment for the delivery of parts," the Merchant spoke in terms of the law of commercial enterprise.

"Will those tradesmen make delivery to you?" the Master continued to develop the plan.

"Upon payment," the Merchant reinforced.

"Then secure delivery of the materials and make payment to the tradesmen," was the Master's obvious instruction.

"But the tradesmen have forced the Blacksmith into an Arrangement and he has no money," alerted the Merchant.

"Are you in an Arrangement?" challenged the Master.

"No Sire," admitted the Merchant.

"Then make payment", demanded the Master.

"You put me in the shoes of the Blacksmith," complained the Merchant.

"No. You both will hang in your own shoes if you disobey," the Master corrected.

"Then I wish to surrender my interest in the Arrangement," the Merchant tried to renege.

"For a fee," the Master bargained.

"Am I to pay for property I will never own and offer service in an Arrangement I did not make?" the Merchant dared to object.

"Yes," was the Master's simple answer.

While the Merchant's fate was sealed other tradesmen remained at large.

Logic does not guide the Master's opinions. His precedents are result oriented outcomes piled on top of prior arbitrary outcomes. Old precedents serve as foundation for new precedents but do not change the outcome. Logic is meaningless in a legal system based upon absolute power. Logic can not explain how a capricious mind dabbles in reason.

From this day forward the Master's precedent established that an Arrangement will bind third parties doing business with the Citizen in debt. All the Citizen's agreements become property of the Arrangement. Every person in contract with a Citizen in debt is a party to the Arrangement. The Court can assume contracts as thought they are property of the Arrangement and impose those agreements on whomever the Court deems appropriate and without consent. After today all contracts have a silent partner - the Court. After today the Court can take a Citizen's contracts without compensation and give the benefit of those contracts to a person of the Court's choosing. Necessity is the mother of all power whereas reason is just an excuse.

When there is no logic to precedents they are impossible to oppose. Precedents are better accepted than understood. The Master's power is absolute therefore his precedents are limitless. One fact in an unlimited outcome has infinite possibilities. While the Master's precedents appear to be arbitrary they conceal a hidden pattern. Even a broken clock is right twice a day whereas an arbitrary precedent conceals the real time. Precedent without reason is folly disguised as power. Folly is a fool's gimmick in betrayal of duty. Duty combats tyranny like loyalty foils treason. For now Citizens are too busy surviving to challenge injustice.

Swindling the Swindler

The Merchant returned to Geoff's shop to explain the precedent. All of Geoff's agreements with other tradesmen were to become property of the Arrangement. The Merchant now stood in Geoff's shoes with authority to enforce his contacts. Geoff worked for the Merchant and all motors belonged to the Court. Parts and materials would be supplied to the Merchant. Payment for parts would be made by the Court once machines were sold and delivered. Tradesmen were ordered to do business with the Merchant as though he was Geoff. All tradesmen with knowledge of the design must reveal those secrets to the Merchant.

Geoff collapsed in despair. Everything he had worked for was taken from him. He was little more than a slave.

"Why should I work under such terms?" Geoff challenged.

"For the same reason you draw your next breath," the Merchant simplified.

"Maybe I'll hold my breath," Geoff protested.

"Maybe you'll wake up with the same problems," the merchant exposed the reality of the situation.

"How am I to make the Mathematician give me his drawings?" Geoff proposed.

"By trickery!" was the Merchant's solution.

"Laudanum?" Geoff queried.

"No. Through false pride," the Merchant revealed his plot.

"The Mathematician is smart, not proud," Geoff argued against the plan.

"All men are proud of being smart," the Merchant countered.

"You think he is so smart he will just give us his design?" Geoff questioned in sarcasm.

"We'll ask for a new design to a bigger machine," the Merchant proposed.

"How will that help?" Geoff didn't understand.

"The Mathematician will have to show us the new drawings before we approve his design," the Merchant assured.

"What then, we steal the drawings?" Geoff doubted.

"You can't steal what belongs to the Master," the Merchant concluded.

"Let the Mathematician produce the drawings so we can tell the Court they exist," conspired the Merchant.

The plot was hatched. The Merchant was empowered by the Court to lie, cheat, and steal. No limit of debauchery obstructed his ruse. An Officer of the Court is forgiven in advance for their illicit acts before they commit them.

Animus in the Object

The burden of maintaining terror in the Star Chamber wore on the Master. He ruled by fear out of quest for unity not only to be cruel. The Realm could not afford diversity. Everyone had to belong to the same Class of underlings. Everyone had to obey the Master if there was to be peace.

The Master knew of the Animus in the Object - terror in the Star Chamber, Zeitgeist in the village, passion in the forest. He did everything possible to distract attention from the Animus in the Object so Citizens would focus on him and not on natural powers. He feared he would be discovered as a puppet and not the puppeteer. He was ambiguous to avoid prediction. He was capricious so as to confuse. He was illogical in order to deny rebuttal. He was a bigot so as to appear equally prejudiced against everyone. The Animus in the Object moved the Master like a storm shapes the countryside - wild yet organized.

If the Master was more sadistic his power would be secure. The masses want to be led because anarchy demands equality that Citizens are not willing to share. The ungoverned predate into self-destruction or unite in self-respect whereas the governed do as told.

The Animus is like the collective conscious of man. Too much oppression breeds bad dreams - for both the oppressed and oppressor. Out of balance minds breed out of balance times. An oppressed Animus reflects back like bad luck. The danger in uniting disturbed minds is that progress is sacrificed for the sake of obedience.

The Master has no theory of leadership, just random quirks instilling fear of reprisal. He does not benefit from history because he does not study it. He does not know the truth because he does not seek it. He can not fashion equity because he does not share power. He can not do justice because he is not at peace. He will not change because he does not realize change is coming. He is simply powerful, like the Animus in the Object.

Members

Members have one code of ethics - help the Court to help themselves. They boast about victimizing their clients. The more demeaning the story the more other Members pay attention. Stories of violating a client's trust satisfy a shared lust between Members. The more private the revelation the more enduring the interest. The mention of money hidden in a woman's undergarment draws arousal. Members live to gossip even though the Master frowns on it because it exposes the exploitation.

> "When I told her the Arrangement would cost twenty coin she broke down into tears," the Member told the gathering of other Members.

> "Did she pay?" another Member inquired.

> "Not with coin," they all broke into laughter.

> "I often take my fee in kind," another Member confirmed the practice.

> "How kind of you," everyone laughed again knowing exactly how the fee was paid.

Members knew they were privileged. They did not think they were superior, that would require talent. They just knew they could get away with anything in an Arrangement. They could take property from one Citizen and give it to another.

They could switch contracts between unwilling parties making a Citizen obligated to perform as never agreed to. Members could have debt forgiven at the expense of everything a Citizen owned. They could substitute their fees for all kinds of illicit payment. The scenarios were limitless and so was the pain and suffering they visited upon Citizens.

Members ignored Citizen misery like the well fed ignore the starving. Members believed that misery of others was necessary for Members' privileges. Without miserable Citizens Members had no status in the Realm. Citizens will be obedient until they revolt. They won't revolt until survival in roaming bands outweighs the benefits of village life. As long as a foreign invader threatens the Realm the Master's oppression is tolerated.

Members didn't design the misery, they just facilitated it. Designing misery took talents that put them in in conflict with the Master. Designing misery requires that you steal your victim's soul. Designing misery takes empathy - understanding the oppressed. It marries cruelty with passion to help those you hurt. Stirring these complex emotions lends charisma to the manipulator but attracts suspicion from the Master. Anyone who could move a crowd was a danger to the Realm.

Members were content occupying their niche. They had seen too many colleagues banished for insubordinence. They had an Ethics Code to uphold which required loyalty to the Court. Citizens did not trust the Ethics Code. Ethics and the law mix like hate and love, one is based on the failure of the other.

Citizens

Not so merry Citizens lived in ignorance of how good life could have been. They toiled from sun up to sun down slipping further into debt. Almost all were forced into an Arrangement at one time or another. Those who could not afford the fees offered their first born son in service of the army. Few conscripts escaped service without being wounded, maimed, or killed.

Life as a Citizen was dismal. Work and debt was a Citizen's fate. The Master and Members kept it that way, with the help of Money Lenders. Money Lenders charged low interest for loans but the penalties took Citizens by surprise. After the first default Money Lenders renegotiated the loan at several times the original interest. After the second default Money Lenders repossessed collateral without extinguishing the debt. After the third default Money Lenders forced Citizens into Arrangements.

Master, Members, and Money Lenders, each contributed to the enterprise of slavery. It started out benign enough. Money was lent for a promise to repay. But the money was impossible to repay and the promise could not be broken. Citizens were expected to go into debt to become prosperous. If Citizens did not borrow they were not ambitious and were not considered loyal to the Realm. If Citizens did not repay their debts they became an outcast. Life in the Realm was predicated on debt. Borrow or perish. Repay or be banished.

The only way to beat the spiral into an Arrangement was

to save. With saved money Citizens could repay their loans and keep what property they borrowed to buy. But Citizens could not buy anything with saved money. Merchants only accepted payment for goods with credit. Citizens could only spend saved money on repaying a loan.

Money Lenders were the middlemen to all commercial transactions. Money Lenders had a special relationship with the Master. They had power second to none. Both the Master and Money Lenders knew not to challenge the others' authority. They negotiated a peace consummated by the Master's power to tax.

The Master charged taxes on debt collected by Money Lenders. Each loan was initiated with a fee paid to the Realm. Money saved for a loan paid taxes instead. Once debt and taxes exceeded net worth Citizens quit borrowing and the economy grew weaker. Citizens quit spending because all money was in the hands of the Master, Members, and Money Lenders. Only a rebellion could end the exploitation.

Money Lenders

Money Lenders were a secretive Class. They kept records on every Citizen, whether in debt or not. They appeared to be without a job or purpose in the Realm, roaming villages in stealth to glean opportunities for their next loan. In a more civil society they would be prosecuted for invasion of privacy.

You knew Money Lenders by appearance, not by name. Money Lenders appeared well dressed, confident, and privileged. Money Lenders carried three possessions: coins, a pen, and a Tiny Book which could be hidden in their shoe. The Tiny Book was much more valuable than their coins. I contained the names of Citizens in debt. If you robbed a Money Lender they would easily surrender their coins but defend their Tiny Book to the death. Your name in the Tiny Book was worth more than the money you borrowed.

The Master took note of the Money Lenders' effort to gather information. The Master contemplated how information about Citizens could be used against them. The Master maintained power through punishment. He did not appreciate the connection between information and a Citizen's good behavior. Fees and fines were the currency of the Judiciary, not a Citizen's dependability.

The closest the Master came to valuing information was to tax it. The Master taxed Money Lenders making the loans not Citizens receiving the money. Money Lenders were happy to collect taxes in exchange for their exclusive franchise to lend. In approving this privilege the Master discovered that all other Classes could be taxed as well. Permission to live in the Realm was sanctioned by the Master's power to tax.

Once a year all Citizens paid a tax to belong to a Class. The tax gave Citizens status. The tax also gave permission for one Class to act prejudicially against another. Prejudice helped enforce order. Order instilled peace. Peace promoted obedience. The only threat to peace, order, and obedience was prosperity.

The Master enlisted Money Lenders to insure that debt stifled prosperity. Prosperity causes chaos because it alleviates slavery. Debt, Arrangements, and Class adhesion are the hallmarks of repression. Without these restraints Citizens behave as Individuals. Either the Master or Citizens win this war but it must be fought.

Soldiers

Soldiers are a privileged Class. They exhibit unquestioned loyalty and obedience. Obedience is not a choice in self expression, it is a necessity in battle. Obedience to tactics and loyalty to others in your ranks insures survival against the enemy. An Individual on the battle field is a dead man but five Soldiers abreast attack like a lion.

While the Master reaches an uneasy cooperation with Money Lenders he fears Soldiers. Soldiers are immune to propaganda because battle is the ultimate proof of life. Facing death frees mortal men of earthly fears. Soldiers are not to be trifled with.

The most dangerous of Soldiers are Nobles who serve with duty. Nobles are exposed to ordinary Soldiers transformed into heros by battle. Nobles learn from these Citizen Soldiers that unearned privilege is a curse. Unearned privilege is despised. A despised Soldier ought to defect to the enemy where his chance of survival is greater.

Soldiers who win respect in the ranks also win respect at home. These natural leaders know how to inspire fellow Citizens. A man of the people leads by example. Soldiers guard their reputation like a medal of honor - an example for all to follow.

The Master carefully watches the ranks for effective leaders. Strong military men must be exiled to distant campaigns or co-opted into government. The Master can't risk letting a Soldier maneuver the crowd. Once a Citizen becomes a Soldier they become empowered. Once a Noble becomes a Soldier they become united with other Citizens. An empowered Soldier is a threat to tyranny. The tyrannical Master is a threat to Citizens. A standing army is a threat to the Master. The Master perpetuates this cycle by unifying power with tyranny in a threat against all Citizens.

The Modality of Truth

Citizens felt betrayed. They knew they should not be treated like slaves. Slaves are a conquered people who are forced into labor. Citizens on the other hand willingly accept their station in the Realm. There is a Social Contract between Citizens and the Master. If that Contract is broken there is no trust binding Citizens to the Realm. If that Contract is violated Citizens lose all advantages to civil organization.

Citizens began discussing their plight. Some knew their discussions were seditious. Others didn't care. Still others plotted to overthrow the Master.

Citizens forced into Arrangements knew they had been cheated. They were subjected to the arbitrary outcomes and knew it was not Justice. Justice promotes equity not folly. Justice maintains the peace not the conflict.

"The Master takes our property unfairly," starts the criticism.

"He rules by fear and threatens our families," another Citizen complains.

"He is not that strong and can be overthrown," the brave reply.

"We must use Arrangements against him," they realize.

The idea of rebellion is self-fulfilling. The idea causes the effect. The word demands action. Rebellion forms a crowd like history begins an epoch. One is made for the other. Rebellion is the "Now" in motion. When the crowd rebels the outcome gives Revolution its meaning. Action defines understanding and a truth is born. Truth must be obeyed.

"We must use Arrangements against him," echoed their realization.

No one knew how to end slavery but they believed taking action was key to their freedom. The Citizens dispersed to continue their discussions another day.

Surprise of Practicality

Geoff proposed the idea of building a bigger motor to the Mathematician. Geoff told the Mathematician he had permission from the Court to attempt any strategy to work his way out of debt. A bigger motor would create bigger profits. Pumping more water meant more crops could be produced with less labor. Anyone could see that bigger was better.

The Mathematician declined to help design a bigger machine. He said the current motor could not be enlarged. A bigger pump must run faster and would break easier. It was not so simple as increasing the size of everything. New calculations must be performed. New methods must be invented. New tests must be carried out. Only a well funded business could afford the risk of developing a bigger machine.

Geoff actually felt relieved by the Mathematician's discouragement. Geoff was comfortable building his old machine. He could do it in his sleep. Farmers were happy with its performance and he could still sell every irrigation motor he built. Geoff's current methods were practical. The trick was making them profitable.

Geoff made one last proposal to the Mathematician. Geoff assured the Mathematician Geoff would perish if he did not expand. Geoff must double production or go out of business. Geoff offered to purchase the Mathematician's drawings. Geoff wanted to employ the Sculptor and Potter to make molds at Geoff's shop. Geoff would take control over all means of production. Instead of waiting for parts to arrive from other tradesmen Geoff would produce what he needed in his own shop.

The Mathematician liked Geoff's plan. Geoff's problems were organizational not structural. Geoff's machines worked and he knew how to build them. By making all parts himself no single step would hold up production. When problems arose Geoff could fix them instead of waiting for others with different schedules to respond. Plus, there would be no more debt. Geoff would pay himself to build what he contracted with others to supply.

Geoff's next task was to recruit the Sculptor and Potter to work for Geoff. These two craftsmen were more artisans than tradesmen. They kept unusual hours, sometimes sleeping all day and working all night. They were not inclined to work in Geoff's dirty smoky shop, or work at all in the traditional sense. Geoff wondered if the Merchant's laudanum would help solicit these artists.

Geoff summonsed the Sculptor and Potter to explain his dilemma. Geoff informed them he now owned the Mathematician's drawings and must double production. Geoff asked whether the Potter and Sculptor would work for him. They both declined. They already had day jobs dreaming up their next inspiration. They only worked at night if they worked at all.

Geoff asked if they had apprentices. They both did.

Geoff inquired if their apprentices could be hired. The artists were glad to shed responsibility for their apprentices because these trainees did not like working late into the night.

Geoff now owned his design, had employees, and controlled his means of production. He was not the same Blacksmith who was forced into an Arrangement but he was still indebted to the Merchant. Geoff needed to renegotiate his agreement with the Merchant and dismiss his Arrangement with the Court.

Scarlet "A" For Arrangement

Word got out Geoff was in an Arrangement. Citizens were afraid to look his way in fear they might catch his disease. Geoff felt the stigma of their distrust. His reputation was tarnished. He worried customers would stop buying irrigation motors. He was angry at being made a slave when he had a realistic plan to repay his debts.

Other Citizens in Arrangements stopped by Geoff's shop to compare their situations. Once Citizens began comparing notes they realized how corrupt the Master was. They all complained but none would act. They looked to Geoff for answers.

Geoff was uncomfortable representing others in Arrangements. He was a Blacksmith not an orator. He was trained in metalwork not in leading rebellions. Nonetheless he was the leader the crowd wanted. He was strong, direct, and honest. The Mathematician and Merchant realized Geoff would make the ideal proxy.

The Mathematician and Merchant hatched a plan to revolt against the Master. They recruited disenfranchised Citizens to protest the Master's exploitation. They held meetings in Geoff's shop to discuss repealing Arrangements. The meetings looked like a product demonstration. The gatherings appeared to be part of Geoff's Arrangement to sell more machines. Before each meeting the Mathematician and Merchant coached Geoff how to sway the crowd.

"There are dozens of them and they all are as mad as you," the Merchant prodded Geoff.

"Tell them you can't take it any longer," the Mathematician simplified Geoff's task.

"They will follow you like shadows follow the sun," the Merchant assured.

"What drives them to revolt?" Geoff challenged the Merchant's theory.

"The same as you - slavery," the Mathematician knew their motives.

"They want to act. They just don't have a plan," the Merchant encouraged.

"Let them know you are ready to rebel and they will follow," the Mathematician knew from experience.

"What do I say?" Geoff was still unsure.

"Start by explaining how your machine is the key to your survival," the Merchant directed.

"Tell them how the Master took your invention for the Court to own and Members to sell", the Mathematician tried to provoke Geoff.

"Tell them the Court is corrupt when it takes property belonging to another."

Geoff began felling confident. He wanted to help others as much as himself. He wasn't going to let the Master violate laws of nature. It was unnatural for the Court to take Geoff's invention and divide the proceeds among Members. It was unnatural for the Court to substitute strangers for the real parties to Geoff's agreements. It was unnatural for the Court to extinguish Geoff's debt for a fee once he had a plan to repay. It was unnatural for the Master to conduct Court in such secrecy.

The Merchant and Mathematician knew they must tread lightly. If they weren't careful they would be undone by their own plot.

On the Precipice

The Merchant was a foreigner. He knew several languages and many cultures and he knew oppression when he saw it. He was surprised the Master tolerated his presence. The Master had closed the boarders to the Realm long ago.

The Merchant was not adverse to Revolution, it was good for business. He already supplied the army with ladanum and Devil's Spice. Devil's Spice energized Soldiers on long marches and ladanum subdued their tensions in camp.

The Merchant concealed his subversive talents under cover of his trade. He was witnessing a Realm on the verge of revolt. He knew that change was coming and it would be violent. He knew the oppressed must strike first before the Master struck them. The Merchant thought he could secure a position in the new government if he helped Geoff manipulate Citizens into rebellion.

The formula for Revolution is simple. Once Citizens are provoked they must act with overwhelming force. They must attack on several fronts and appear to be unrelenting because uncompromising fervor wins swift surrender.

The Revolution must simultaneously attack the House of Government, the Court, and Citadel. The Citadel is the tricky part. Executed correctly the Citadel can be conquered bloodlessly. Attack the House of Government, sack the Court, and then surround the Citadel and the army will stay in its barracks. The army knows the next government needs as much protection as the last. It helps if all these targets are in close proximity in the Capitol.

It takes mean provocation to aggravate Citizens to revolt. It also takes a righteous cause to keep the reactionaries at home. The counter-revolutionaries must be quieted else they will become the next revolutionaries. Ultimately the Revolution must accommodate the reactionaries, the sooner the better. Accommodation is a good thing because it legitimizes the Revolution. Ideally the plan for appeasement is in place all along.

After the first bloodshed mercy can spare survivors. Adversaries must be rehabilitated not punished. Sometimes re-education takes a lifetime. Those quick to rehabilitate can serve as model Citizens eager to denounce their uninformed past. Those slow to rehabilitate can serve as examples confined to special institutions.

Darkness in the Star Chamber leads to Darkness in the Revolution if the goals are not clear. Old icons become new icons if the message is corrupt. Revolution can either cleanse or destroy - like a thunderstorm.

Seeds of Revolution

History is a battle over ideas. "Right for might", "to each according to their needs", "racial purity", and "free enterprise". Each idea has shared time with history. Governments are easy to topple because they are built on ideas. It doesn't take much insurrection to topple an idea because most history is revisionist fiction. The bloodshed doesn't change only the reason does. History does not repeat itself because that would require time travel.

History is an evolution of conflict. The thesis is in conflict with the anti-thesis - synthesizing a new thesis, and so on and so on. Old ideas evolve into new ideas without remaining the same. The past does not limit the future. War accelerates invention and progress is the byproduct.

History doesn't care if Citizens think it repeats itself or if they believe one phase synthesizes the next. Historians don't predict the future else they would be busy avoiding the next calamity. Only the "Now" offers potential for change. The Now is not bound to the past or future. It is the truest expression of time, going nowhere while being forced into the moment. In that stillness all is possible.

Revolution is the vehicle for judicial reform. All Revolutions overthrow sitting Courts. While the bloodbath is fought to take possession of Government the real prize is in taking possession of the Court. It is the Court that provokes the Revolution by ignoring it. Governments are normally inept, the more inept the better. Courts on the other hand are never inept. Justice may be fickle but she is never indifferent. The greatest danger comes when the Court merges with the Government.

Revolutionary change must be instantaneous. If change happens too slowly the past corrupts the future. If change happens too fast the last phase can not evolve into the next. If the Revolution happens instantaneously there is no time to pervert its principles

The next idea waiting to change the Realm was already under way. That idea was a Meme in the Mirror looking back like the mind see the face. After that idea becomes known a leader must transform it into change. Manifesting an idea whose time has come into the Now requires skill. The Masters spends a fortune suppressing ideas that are poised to change the Realm.

Recognizing the next great idea requires focus - like studying addition. 2 + 2 equals — quick — 3! It doesn't matter if you are right or wrong because great ideas are neither. The answer is not important - the question is. It doesn't matter if 2 + 2 = 3 because 2 x 2 = 4. Use what works.

There is an idea Citizens are waiting to learn that will change their future - but what is it. Citizens must first assume the idea is true then try to disprove it. They must assume they know the next great idea and live their lives trying to disprove they are right. The Mathematician, Merchant, and Blacksmith were about to employ this powerful proof.

The Right Idea

The Right Idea is like a friend waiting for you to arrive, it gets there before you. It's like hearing music no one is playing, it exists without you. The Right Idea has a spirit all its own, your are ITS agent. The Right Idea spontaneously combusts. You can fight the fire but you can't fight the cause.

The Right Idea should be accepted by passive avoidance. To accept the Right Idea is to realize it is separate from you, something you do not own. To reject the Right Idea is to mistakenly think it was yours to discard to begin with. Once you accept the Right Idea the two of you can begin to support each other.

You empower the Right Idea by acting on its premise. If the Right Idea was self-evident then reality would be a mere illusion, never needing to be challenged. The Right Idea takes work. The Right Idea also has the advantage. Stand back and let the Right Idea have its way with the universe. Assume something powerful is about to happen.

The Right Idea creates its own momentum like space creates time. The Right Idea will run you over if you do not run with it. Geoff felt the Animus in the idea, energy in the Revolution, history in the making. He realized he did not need to fully understand the Right Idea, he only needed to act on it.

Once Geoff realized the Revolution existed despite his understanding he was at ease persuading others to revolt. He used to struggle with his plight but now knew the Revolution made its own opportunity regardless of his apprehension. The outcome was not his to control - it belonged to history.

All knowledge is a belief. We believe that reality is not an illusion but we can not prove it. We believe that numbers are real when they are only symbols. We believe in evolution but can't see it. We believe in God but haven't met Her. To mistake belief for knowledge is to mistake illusion for reality when they are one in the same.

School

Geoff threw open the doors to his shop for all to visit. He began teaching others the secrets of his trade. The Merchant and Mathematician offered lessons in business and design. Citizens attended classes on negotiating more favorable Arrangements. Tradesmen with other skills shared their knowledge as well. What once was a closed shop shrouded in secrecy became a meeting place open for sharing knowledge. In that exchange a School was born.

School is the Right Idea. It is as compelling as food and water. School has spirit, momentum, and evolution. It can be subverted yet it is also subversive - enlightening. Left to cultural ambitions School liberates. Left to political ambitions School regiments.

School is the Right Idea for battling oppression. A learned mind resists slavery like the righteous resist corruption. One informed question leads to another. A question in mathematics leads to a question about Justice. All knowledge is related. When the mind is schooled it creates new knowledge by seeking it.

Geoff observed that students make good Citizens. Once educated it is harder to reject the obvious. The problem is the obvious gets harder to educate. Knowledge piles up and appears to be infinite. Infinity is something you have to believe in to know. At some point students must take a leap of faith. They must believe that actions speak louder than words.

The danger of education is that knowledge gives rise to action. Education is also destabilizing because there is so much to learn. The smartest people know what they do don't know, which is a lot. Learned discipline requires balancing competing values: belief with knowledge, action with restraint, myth with the pursuit of Justice. Fortunately to ask is to answer.

Geoff had a home but lived in his shop because he worked such long hours. His shop was dangerous so he opened his home for others to hold classes. He now had two jobs - Blacksmith and host. He enjoyed hosting classes. It put him in contact with his rarest encounter - women. He had a lot to tell them but nothing to do with irrigation motors. He discovered his charm was a great elixir, better than ladanum. When he spoke passionately about ending Arrangements everyone listened.

One woman in particular caught Geoff's eye. Her name was Ann. She worked in the fields and was as strong as Geoff, but more elegant and agile. Geoff saw her lift a frail student in the palm of her hand, without grasping more closely with her full body. Ann attended the Mathematician's classes. She taught herself how to calculate the area of a circle. She knew the weight of water, thickness of paper, and that time and distance were synonymous. She also realized knowledge was a curse, something Courts punish witches for possessing.

Most Citizens attended classes to get ahead. A few attended just to attend, for something to do. Still fewer attended for the sake of knowledge. Ann attended school to develop her theory of numbers. She had discovered a new way of counting with equations nested inside other equations. She showed the Mathematician her new system and he told her to keep it a secret. He realized her methods would speed up most calculations. Her processes would make interest on money more valuable, Arrangements more efficient, and machines quicker to design. Some might harm her to learn the rules of her calculations.

Geoff conducted classes on Arrangements every week. Citizens attended just to belong to his group. Geoff covered all aspects of life in the Realm because everything was related to debt. Classes overflowed out of his house and onto his yard. Classes got so large that people lined the road to his property. Geoff was becoming famous and a threat to the Master and Arrangements.

The Merchant and Mathematician encouraged Geoff to change his message from docile instruction to direct insurrection.

"A lingering crowd wastes its purpose," the Merchant advised Geoff.

"Inaction spoils the lesson," the Merchant warned.

"The people have never been so happy," Geoff argued for reconsideration.

"They enjoy learning," Geoff confirmed.

"They haven't learned the Master's plan," the Merchant rebutted.

"Once the Master retaliates you will never hold class again," the Merchant assured.

"Am I to disrupt the peace by striking first?" Geoff rejected the thought of preemptive force.

"Strike first or be stricken," the Merchant affirmed.

In a personal disclosure Geoff changed the subject, "I think I have a chance at marriage".

"A short lived chance I assure you," the Merchant spoiled the news.

"Why are you so opposed to my happiness?" Geoff challenged.

"To avoid your sadness," the Merchant countered.

"Let me live my life," Geoff complained.

"Life in an Arrangement is not worth living," the Merchant reminded.

Geoff completed the circle of despair by returning to the prime directive, "Life in an Arrangement is not worth living." His options were obvious. Rebellion was no longer a choice - it was a necessity.

The Master's Retaliation

The Master grew suspicious of Geoff's activities. The crowds, meetings, and school were not part of the Blacksmith's Arrangement. The Master's capricious precedents were intended to enslave Citizens - not enlighten them. The Master must not lose control over forcing Citizens into poverty. A Master who does not educate must subjugate.

The Master summonsed Members, Money Lenders, and Soldiers to suppress the rebellion. They were his loyal Subjects. They relied on the Master who depended on them. One gave support to the other. Spies were recruited to infiltrate the rebellion. Soldiers were chosen for this task because of their reconnaissance skills. They were told to dress in plain clothes and attend class at Geoff's shop. They were instructed to pay closest attention to who whispered in Geoff's ear.

The Master prepared Members and Money Lenders for a more clandestine conspiracy. Formal charges would be prepared against rebellious Citizens in advance of collecting evidence.

"You already know the charges," the Master informed Members.

"Now make up the evidence," the Master instructed.

The Master directed Money Lenders to retaliate as well.

"Find out who belongs to the rebellion and call in their

loans," the Master ordered.

"We'll force them all into Arrangements," the Master plotted to retake control.

The Master increased his public appearances, rallying the faithful and warning Citizens of traitors among them. He whipped the masses into a counter-revolutionary frenzy, readying them for the coming cleansing. His words stirred demons within the crowd. Scapegoating innocent victims satisfied perverse fantasies.

"Do not guard the Realm for my sake," the Master pled with the crowd, clutching air in both fists, drawing them close to his chest, staring skyward for inspiration.

"Hunt the traitors to preserve the future for your children and their safety," the Master distracted from himself, pointing over the crowd.

"Nothing threatens the Real more than treason," the Master blamed the anonymous perpetrators, grasping fists of air again.

"The criminals must be brought to justice," the Master demanded, snapping the neck of an imaginary traitor in front of him.

"You'll know them when you see them," the Master offered vague guidance, appearing to smooth a sand berm with the gentle sweep of his hand.

"They disobey the law by acting guilty," the Master describes innocent behavior worth punishing.

"They run when chased," the Master identified the prey, pretending to follow them into the distance when pursued.

"They violate Arrangements because they are guilty of treason," the Master lent reason to his excuse, pointing his finger directly at the crowd.

"No one will miss them at trial," the Master gave permission to violate their rights, shaking his head to minimize their value.

"Once Arrangements are obeyed we will be safe again," the Master shared his vision, exploding in jubilation.

The crowd erupted in cheers. They united against a common enemy that did not exist. They looked upon one another as their next trophy to persecute. Everyone was a potential traitor. Only the vicious would survive.

"I can tell you where the traitors dwell," the Master confides in the crowd.

"Some are your neighbors, some are your friends, " the Master prepares the crowd for the unthinkable.

"Some are mothers and fathers, some are husbands and wives," the Master begins to test their allegiance.

"Will you bring them to justice?" the Master unleashes the hounds.

The Master ends abruptly, leaving the podium without further provocation. He has not given the crowd a clear order to follow. He leaves them free to act out their own vendetta. Their imaginations harbor more malice than his words can provoke. The crowd's capacity for crimes is not limited by the Master's vague aspersions. He is the facilitator not a participant. The crowd has demons which the Master does not fully understand or control.

The crowd disperses, dissatisfied with its instructions. Like hyenas interrupted from the feast they search for a fresh meal. Someone in the crowd will be beaten tonight but no one knows who or why.

The Master chose three Soldiers as spies. In private he instructs them to spy on each other as well as to spy on Geoff and the rebels. Being trained in surveillance taught them there was always a spy spying on the spy. They knew if they were told to spy on one another there must be a spy spying on them. Soldiers play spy like the cat stalks the mouse, it's both a game and dinner.

Every now and then the cat surprises its prey by releasing the catch. Such is the price of domestication - honor among predators. Many Soldiers served in the army as payment for their parents' Arrangements. Their Class origins ran thick in their blood. Their family bonds transcended ideology. Faced with betraying their roots or betraying the Master they can not deny their upbringing.

Such was the Master's dilemma - rely on Soldiers from the most oppressed Class or rely on other Citizens not as well trained. The effect of training on obedience was easy to judge, the Master could tell when it was insufficient. The effect of oppression on obedience was harder to judge because all Citizens are potential traitors. The Master had to take his chances with Soldiers but he did not trust them.

"Your mother is the army now and your father is the Realm," the Master began inducting spies into his service.

"Your parents no longer nurture you," the Master substitutes his care for their parents' love.

"You must find kinship with the Realm," the Master proposes their adoption.

"Duty binds your new family," the Master enlists their loyalty.

"I will protect you with my life," the Master makes a false promise in exchange for their commitment.

"If you will sacrifice your life for the Realm," the Master discloses his plan for using them.

"Let us join in a pact of honor," the Master inspires their highest ambitions.

"Let us honor what only we can create," the Master unites his Clan.

"Serve with purpose, pride, and permission," the Master hints at their special privileges.

"No authority will limit your judgment," the Master introduces the bargain.

"If you will not limit your authority," the Master unleashes their restraint.

"One Clan, One Purpose, One Rule," the Master finished in a crescendo.

"Men of the Realm, for Security, without Bounds," was their mantra.

The Master gave his new Clan a name - **FISA**, which stood for **F**ellow **I**nternal **S**ecurity **A**gents. He created a special Court which met in secrecy to conduct its business. No records were kept, no evidence collected, no allegations raised. Only unsubstantiated rumors carried the weight of prosecution. The Master wondered if the rebellion wasn't his greatest ally.

The trap was set. The stakes were high. Some knew the game was being played, others were about to find out. The outcome was anything but certain.

The Address

A large crowd gathered on Geoff's lawn to attend his class. The entire village was present, including spies. The Master attended disguised as a homeless vagrant. Money Lenders and Members were easy to spot by their formal attire. Soldiers attended in uniform as a reminder not to cross the line. The Merchant and Mathematician sat behind the Blacksmith to lend support. Ann was closest to Geoff's side.

Geoff stepped up onto a small makeshift platform elevated slightly above the crowd, under the shade cloth stretched from tree limb to limb. His yard was on a gentle hill forming the perfect amphitheater. As he began to speak the crowd kneeled to rest upon their coats and blankets spread about the law. Chattering song birds quieted, remaining silent throughout his presentation. The moment belonged to Geoff.

"Freedom is a right," Geoff began his rally.

"Debt is slavery," Geoff contended.

"At first you borrow to be free then debt overtakes you," Geoff exposed the contradiction.

"Progress and prosperity are replaced by debt," Geoff observed.

"The Master redirects debt payment to himself through Arrangements," Geoff disclosed the trick.

"Debt is a hidden tax," Geoff described the scheme.

"Debt repaid to storekeepers builds our markets," Geoff pronounced the obvious.

"Debt diverted to the Master only builds his power," Geoff teetered on treason.

"We can forgive our own debt," Geoff challenged the received wisdom.

"We are our own Masters," Geoff introduced a new theology.

"We are the source of our own power," Geoff dared to propose such a revolutionary idea.

"Save and purchase what you need with your own money," Geoff encouraged new responsibility.

"The Master can not tax the coins in your pocket," Geoff denounced.

"And if he does he is a thief," Geoff crossed the line.

Believers jumped to their feet in applause. Subjects loyal to the Master whispered in disagreement. Spies rushed the stage to arrest Geoff for sedition. A melee erupted between loyalists on each side. Brawling combatants fought indiscriminately. You couldn't tell who was fighting for who. In the commotion

Geoff escaped under escort by the Merchant and Mathematician, leaving the crowd pitched in battle.

So few words caused such violence. The fight was not over ideas, it was over prejudices. The idea of debt forgiveness had too little meaning to cause a fight because the Master controlled its ambiguous practice. But Citizens understood what being their own Master meant. Being your own Master was worth fighting for - and against. Some worried if Citizens were their own Master then who would control their neighbors? If Citizens were their own Master then who would be the most powerful?

Geoff's call for self-empowerment threatened the status quo. The idea of transferring power from the Master to Citizens was traumatic. Change was disruptive. Security depended on stability.   Fear of the unknown had always cemented the Master's power in the past. Challenging that fear required force.

Geoff In Exile

Geoff fled to the forest in exile. A stream of followers gave his location away but they also provided protection. His retreat was tactical not permanent. Withdrawing from conflict saved lives and strengthened his influence. The longer he survived the further his message spread. Time was on his side.

Believers rallied around Geoff and readied for battle. Geoff took inspiration from wolves in the forest for his tactics. Wolves surround their prey sealing its escape. They attack with overwhelming force and disperse after the kill. Geoff organized his troops in small groups, like wolf packs. Their small numbers concealed their lethal potential. They entered the Capitol as individuals separated from the pack. They approach their target casually, threatening to no one. Then they reform as a group attacking with surprise.

Their first mission was to sack the Court. They circled the perimeter sealing off the building's defense. They set the roof and doors ablaze. They painted the walls with pig's blood declaring "Freedom or Death". Their work was done within minutes. They quickly dispersed without discovery. They effected maximum terror under cover of daylight.

Their next target was the House of Government. Geoff's troops trained for a night attack. They could not risk another daylight raid. Their intent was to terrorize not triumph. Their numbers were too small for victory just yet. They paired off in groups of two comprising a spotter and archer. Archers practiced their skills for a week before the attack. Spotters carried tar, flame, and lit arrows. Dozens of archers launched dozens of flaming arrows in an inferno descending from above. The fire brigade doused the flames before the forest burnt down.

The night of the attack teams of two approached the House of Government from all directions. They dressed in black and hugged the shadows. If discovered they staggered and stumbled mimicking drunken farm hands celebrating the harvest. At the designated time a signalman shot a flaming arrow high above the target. In an instant archers released their volley of fire. Spotters rearmed the archers with freshly lit arrows. Another volley and another lit the sky. The House of Government was set ablaze within seconds. The precision of the archers' marksmanship was faultless. Not an errant missel missed its target. The attackers quickly returned to the forest where a small party protected their retreat. No lives were lost and no witnesses observed the attack.

The next attack was the most dangerous. It would be on the Citadel. The Master knew it was coming and prepared for the bloodbath. He dispatched spies to infiltrate Geoff's troops. Geoff responded in kind and sent volunteers to the Capitol to observe the Master's preparation. Misinformation infected misinformation as each side tried to spoil the other's reconnaissance. It took experts to decipher what may or may not be true. Suspicion hung over each inner circle like rumors of an assassin. Paranoia became the mind set. Strategy became convoluted to deflect surveillance. Elaborate plots were leaked to conceal simple plans. Doubt tainted observation until denial incapacitated good judgment. Nothing was true when everything was known. Both sides prepared for a battle they could not win. A battle conducted under such circumstances would surely result in slaughter.

The Merchant, Mathematician, and Geoff withdrew to a safer place to discuss their plans in private. They were practical strategists, not egotistical mad men. Leading their followers into defeat was not an option. The situation demanded more innovative thinking.

"What if we staged a battle but no one came," Geoff proposed the ridicules.

"What would be the purpose," the Mathematician knew not to dismiss the absurd.

"To give thanks to living," Geoff began outlining his strategy.

"For who," the Merchant challenged.

"For those called upon to die in battle against us ," Geoff reflected.

"You believe fear of death makes a Soldier surrender?" the Merchant questioned the inconsistency.

"Not fear, but satisfaction," Geoff equated apprehension with glory.

"Explain," the Mathematician asked for clarity.

"If we stage a battle that we do not hold then we satisfy the Soldier's duty of loyalty," Geoff imagined, "they are none the less for not fighting and dying".

"Battles aren't won that way," the Merchant objected.

"But the Citizens are never the generals," Geoff replied.

"No - the Soldiers are and they are trained to fight," the Merchant corrected.

"They are trained to serve and obey," Geoff zeroed in on the elements of his challenge.

"Surrender is not an option," the Merchant reminded.

"I'm proposing an obedience to a higher service," Geoff substituted reason in place of doubt.

"To God?" the Merchant scoffed.

"To each other," Geoff offered an alternative.

"OK," the Mathematician considered.

"How do we test your plan without getting killed," was a reasonable question.

"Slowly, and in steps," Geoff felt he knew the answer.

"We stage fake attacks on the Citadel and quickly retreat," Geoff explained.

"After enough attempts Soldiers will wait for our next charge, not believing it will come," Geoff predicted.

"Then we lay down our arms and wait for their surrender," Geoff's plan sounded like suicide.

"And if they charge - what then?" the Merchant had reason to ask.

"We are dead either way," Geoff eliminated the doubt.

"Dead either way?" the Merchant could not deny.

It was an odd way to phrase a battle plan. Geoff's view challenged tradition not reality. Fighting and losing were inevitable just not popular to admit. Geoff's theory certainly took risk off the table for there was nothing left to lose.

The Mathematician liked Geoff's battle plan because it had not been tested. He was accustomed to rearranging terms when balancing an outcome. The answer lay in the process. Stage a fight, appear to retreat, and invite surrender - it had never been tried before. It shifted emphasis off the Soldier's training and onto their roots and upbringing. The Master was just a proxy for the Soldier's need to belong to something more meaningful.

As long as no one challenged the Master then Soldiers were loyal to his delusions. But when challenges became righteous the Master's strangle hold was no match against Citizens' unified revolt. Staging a confrontation was as important for the rebellion as it was for Soldiers entrusted to serve the Master. The sooner the tide turned the fewer would perish.

The rules of military engagement were well established. The rules of rebellion were new. Geoff realized his troops must be trained to execute his new tactic. Any misstep and their retreat would be interpreted as defeat. It was important to stand in place against Soldiers defending the Citadel as long as possible. Geoff needed to deliver the clearest message of defiance that courage could demonstrate. Geoff depended on Soldiers guarding the Citadel to maintain a defensive posture. Geoff must risk they will not charge and give up their advantage. Geoff's troops must approach so closely as to defy cowardice. Their message must be clear, "We will fight and die but we offer you quarter".

There is a danger in demanding blind obedience in battle if you do not anticipate your opponent's surprises. Stand and fight is an easy command when your enemy cooperates by attacking. Defending the Citadel gave the Master the high ground which he would not easily abandon. Geoff felt confident the battle would go as planned.

But Geoff's battle plan could only be known by his most trusted insiders. Spies would foil the effect. Even Geoff's troops were unsure why they trained to attack and sometimes trained to retreat. On the fateful day of confrontation Geoff's plan remained a secret.

At sunrise Geoff closed his camp to visitors to seal it off from spies. He assembled his troops and told them this was to be the day. He guaranteed victory if they would follow his instructions. He didn't deliver an inspiring speech because he wanted to preserve their restraint. Retreat was more important than attack.

"Now quickly, we must march in double step to the edge of the Capitol," was Geoff's only command.

He waited for his troops to form behind him. Then he quickened the pace so spies could not forward a message announcing their approach. At the edge of the Capitol he gave pause before battle, as any seasoned commander would do. This was the first time spies had a chance to sound the alarm. Soldiers in the barracks rushed into formation. Officers took their positions. Geoff waited for the formalities of battle to organize. This was not a surprise attack, that was not its purpose. Geoff wanted the opposition to fully engage. He wanted them to fully contemplate their potential death. The Master withdrew to his balcony overlooking the Citadel. He had a clear view of the battlefield below. He could see Geoff's troops in a slow procession, not anxious to attack. He motioned to his generals to stand firm in a defensive position. Time dilated as minutes seemed like hours.

Finally both armies were within striking range of each

other. Geoff ordered his troops to kneel. He handed his weapons to the next in charge. He approached half way between the two skirmish lines. He turned his back on the Citadel to review his own troops. He then spun around toward the Master up in the balcony. Geoff raised his hand high above his head and made the sign to "halt", palm flat against the wind. He addressed the Master with defiant bravado.

"Abolish Arrangements," echoed into history.

"We are our own Masters," authorized his demand.

"Freedom or Death," was his ultimatum.

The Master delayed in responding. He knew the effect of pause aggravated the stress. He leaned over the balcony appearing to measure the situation. More pause caused more tension. He looked to Geoff and then to his own Soldiers. The Master gestured to his army to brush Geoff off like dust off his boots. He waved both hands outward, quickly and in unison, with palms down, as if fanning flames. His Soldiers gave a collective "hurrah" - more obligatory than sincere. Geoff turned to his own troops. They ascended from their kneeling position. Clatter of weapons emanated from both sides. Posture became erect and mussels flexed. The full frontal standoff between two armies reflected back and forth like a hall of mirrors. Soldiers saw themselves in the other side. Primordial instinct narrowed their field of vision. Hearts pounded, hearing quieted, time stopped. Heroism would be rewarded by survival entrusted to fate. Opposing armies joined in a collective breath, inhaling all the air in their vicinity. With deliberate retrospect Soldiers saw their lives pass quickly before them. Their last moment of consciousness was suspended in memories of glory.

The moment was so intense it was difficult to give commands - for either leader. Geoff felt advantage reinvesting in his strategy. He knew time was speeding by but seemed like in a crawl. He must draw out the moment and wait for it to pass. His troops were captured by time and could barely respond. "Dead either way" echoed across the battlefield.

Geoff slowly withdrew to the middle of his troops so as not to provoke the opposing side. Geoff's troops stepped backward as a unit, still facing the Master's Soldiers. Geoff became the eyes and ears of his troops in retreat, guiding them away from the engagement.

The Master was confused by the maneuver, never having witnessed an attack ending in retreat before the battle began. The Master sensed a trick so he instructed his troops to remain in position and not take the bait. Geoff's plan worked perfectly. The only thing remaining was to measure its effect.

The Assassin

Misinformation intensified on both sides. The Master claimed to have defeated Geoff but no one saw the battle. Geoff had a more diabolical plot in mind.

Geoff spread rumor of a fictitious Assassin preparing to kill the Master. Geoff circulated stories of the Assassin's hero status. The Assassin was willing to risk his life to rid the Realm of the oppressive Master. Citizens in Arrangements were said to be sheltering the Assassin - changing his location daily. There were not enough Soldiers to search all the residences of all the Citizens in Arrangements to find the Assassin. The Assassin remained at large and could strike at will.

"Have you heard of the Assassin," was the topic of conversation.

"I saw him," rumor gave rumor to rumor.

"God's speed to him," disgruntled Citizens prayed for the Assassin's success.

Citizens in Arrangements breathed life into the rumor of the Assassin. He was fearless and invincible. Citizens realized that rumor of the Assassin might shield a real attempt on the Master's life. If the rumored Assassin remained at large then a real assassin could maneuver more freely. Searching for a ghost would distract the Master from locating real assassins.

Three Citizens recognized their opportunity to strike under cover of the rumor. They grew up together. No outsider could infiltrate their confidence without the other knowing about the intrusion. The had total trust in each other. They were the perfect assassins' cell. Closed without being secretive. Active without standing out. Motivated without attracting suspicion. Plus, they had special talents. One was an ex-Soldier, one was a bow maker, and one tinkered in all the other trades. Their bond formed the perfect conspiracy, like a clock set for sunrise - inevitable.

An artist drew a false rendering of the rumored Assassin which Geoff posted in the public square. The Assassin was seen here and there but nowhere. Sightings consumed the Master's spies who were dispatched each time the Assassin was spotted. Citizens asked for a reward for capturing the Assassin but the Master did not want to create a legend. Soon, the Assassin's presence would be felt.

Members, Money Lenders, Soldiers, and spies realized they were at risk. They were all part of the Master's inner circle. If you did not support the rebellion you were against it. If you were not part of the solution you were part of the problem. Rumors circulated there was a bounty on anyone who would not disavow the Master.

Then the real assassins struck. They kidnaped the leading Member of the Master's Court. His disappearance caused more concern than would discovery of his body. A dismembered body satisfied curiosity whereas a missing body could still be tortured.

Other Members could only guess what brutality awaited their fate. Their preoccupation with their own demise paralyze their routine. They could not concentrate on official business. Arrangements grew weaker and more forgiving. The Master was losing his grip.

The real assassins struck a second time, capturing and hanging three Money Lenders. Except the hangings were only staged. The Money Lenders were hung by harnesses concealed under their clothes. A noose was flung over their neck appearing to do the work but the harnesses carried all the weight of their body. They were strung up at night in the public square, kicking and yelling for all to see the next morning. Onlookers wondered why the Money Lenders would not die, never thinking to cut them down to end their misery. The spectacle was too comical to spoil the entertainment.

Only the spies were spared public ridicule. The real assassins knew that spies must be converted, not humiliated. Spies waited to be captured. They set a trap of three, never going into public without escort or observers. They came out of the fold trying to draw the Assassin into the open. They spoke freely of their mission to catch the Assassin hoping to attract his attention. Eventually, everyone knew the spies were spies. Their cover was exposed and their value as spies was little more than a Money Lender. Rumor of the Assassin accomplished its purpose without bloodshed.

Short Lived Peace

Geoff came out of the forest to negotiate peace. Geoff insisted that the Master resign from the Court and surrender all power. He could keep his Palace overlooking the Citadel but the next generals must be appointed by a Tribunal elected by Citizens to govern the Realm.

The Master appeared to accept Geoff's terms of peace, knowing he could violate them at will. The Master did not rule by consensus in the first place and did not respect the concept. His surrender was just a ruse to expose the rebellion. Geoff knew as much but wanted Citizens to taste freedom before the final battle.

Geoff's first official act was to replace the Court with an Oracle. The Oracle consisted of a stone sphere in a wooden box labeled with predetermined outcomes. Adversaries seeking remedy from the Court spun the sphere and waited for it land on a judgment. The Oracle was not logical, or accurate, or even random. It was not meant to satisfy Justice. It was meant to frustrate conflicts. If you found yourself in a conflict needing resolution by the Court you were no better off consulting the Oracle than a game of chance. The Oracle was meant to teach Citizens to resolve their own disputes. It was arbitrary but not exploitive.

In Geoff's plan for the Realm there was only the Law. There was no Court to corrupt the will of the people or change a vote of the Tribunal. Government was not constrained by the separation of powers. Rebellion played that role. Tyranny is too weak a threat when persistent rebellion inspires the Revolution.

Geoff knew his form of utopia was too ideal. He knew the Master would seduce Citizens with promises of privileges and power. Citizens wanted to be free but they also wanted to live like the Master. A new idea for satisfying powerful ambitions needed introduction. Something compelling needed to substitute humility for power. But if that idea became too powerful it would replace the rebellion. An institution somewhere between Divinity and the Tribunal was needed. A concept in between God and Government was required. Geoff realized that Trade Unions must be formed.

Geoff envisioned that workers would lead the rebellion through Trade Unions. Learned Citizens with trade skills would occupy government. Whatever pride and prejudices these new leaders harbored were the same faults that consumed the hearts and minds of their constituents. Elitists with selfish prejudices would not govern, workers with ordinary prejudices would.

The Master waited patiently for folly to replace his absence.

The Master Makes His Move

The real assassins knew their work was not done. They were realists not revolutionaries. They did not prescribe to Tribunals, Courts, or Unions. They knew the Master would counterattack and Citizens would be too busy reorganizing the Realm. Like predators cloaked by their surroundings the real assassins hid under cover of village life, blending in to the vibrant activity of commerce. They watched the Master watch the people.

The Master had trouble recruiting old compatriots. Their lives had been spared by the rebellion and they didn't want to risk double jeopardy. The Master became loud and animated in public when unable to convince ex-loyalists to rejoin his regime. His aggressive behavior attracted attention. When Citizens noticed the Master's boisterous exchanges he dropped the subject and smiled as though discussing old times with friends. The real assassins took notice of the Master's deceit.

The Master resorted to recruiting his most loyal devotee from the past - the hooded Guard to the Star Chamber. The Guard was unknown to the Realm. His hood concealed his true identity. Even Members were not sure who he was. The Guard was the Master's perfect embracery. Without his hood the Guard was ordinary and unremarkable.

The Master and Guard devised a signal code for operating in public. The real assassins could not tell who in the crowd was executing the Master's instructions. The Master would look up, down, or away and lead the Guard to the person of interest. Once identified the Guard would deliver a written message in a swift pass by the person, leaving the recipient unsure where the note came from. Sometimes the note was tied to a rock and thrown at the ex-compatriot's feet. Sometimes the Guard made physical contact in crowded places, dropping the note in their pocket. For more trusted contacts the Guard rushed by, whispering under his breath for the person of interest to look on a nearby table or in the street for the note.

Dozens of contacts were recruited this way until the Master's loyalists could operate more freely in public. Hundreds of faithful Subjects rejoined the Master, happier to disturb the peace than preserve it. Too little bloodshed spilled during the initial rebellion to secure the Revolution's place in history. The Master's new troops respected old fashioned brutality not lucky maneuvering. Their bloodlust was to be satisfied in exchange for their loyalty.

Party Lines

The Revolution and counter-Revolution reformed along party lines - for and against Arrangements. Citizens were only for Arrangements if they had never been in one. No rational person could possibly support turning commerce upside down through Arrangements. Reason could not justify extinguishing debts Citizens could afford to repay. It made no sense to insert strangers into contracts or take property from Citizens and give it to Members. Incarcerating objectors and enriching the Court with fees charged to relieve debt only served the Master, Members, and Money Lenders. Of course they still favored Arrangements. Fortunately there was a shortage of Soldiers willing to sacrifice their lives to protect the scheme. They would stay in their barracks over this fight.

The Master needed to hire some troops. He needed to raid the Treasury to pay his Soldiers. The Treasury had always been funded by Arrangements but Geoff ended Arrangements when he created the Oracle. The only money available to the Realm was through taxation but Geoff sent the tax man home as well. Geoff's plan was to weaken government so it could not become a counter-revolutionary force.

Now it was the Master who was reduced to tactics of sneak attack and retreat. But he had not risen to power that way. Retreat was beneath him. He was the proud Warlord who lead by advance not withdrawal. What would become of War if fought by weasels sneaking into the shed at night? How would Citizens learn to obey if not taught discipline on the battlefield?

Most of all the Master just wanted the money. He was addicted to easy money made off Arrangements. He used to make up the rules which everyone followed. Now the Tribunal made up the rules. Money Lenders lost their exclusive franchise to lend. They no longer had privileges protected by the Court. They had to write contracts that Citizens could fulfill in good faith. Members no longer could bully Citizens into compliance. Members could not litigate their opponents into submission. Law was created and enforced by the Tribunal. The Star Chamber ceased functioning as a place of business where judgments could be bought and sold.

The Master needed a new way to raise revenue. All the normal avenues had been closed by the rebellion. Laws, judgements, and Arrangements were no longer for sale. Taxing the air was no longer an option. The Master had to resort to an outlet he despised when in power - foreign trade. He had prohibited free trade so he could close the boarders. He wanted to keep immigrants out of the Realm. But they snuck in anyway, bringing their culture, skills, and trade.

The Master and his band of highwaymen decided to block the roadways and charge a fee for importing goods into the Realm. They set up on the boarder and charged travelers for permission to pass. They confiscated articles of value from immigrants - threatening the helpless. The Master posed as King and inducted travelers into his service to fight the rebellion. After months of exploiting helpless immigrants the Master was ready to execute a counterattack.

The Rematch

Geoff knew the rematch was coming. He knew the Master was staging a counter attack, just far enough out of reach on the boarder. Geoff did not want to repeat the Master's mistake of over-militarizing life in the Realm so he did not raise a standing army. He knew that the right balance to security lay with a well regulated militia of volunteers not forced into servitude. The Master's old army had already shown tolerance for the Revolution by returning to their barracks after the initial rebellion. Geoff realized that all new institutions needed to pass the test of fire. The sooner it happened the sooner peace prevailed. When the time came Geoff believed Citizen volunteering for the militia would know what to do.

Citizens were happy to spare more bloodshed but the Master was not. For him rebellion must be met with repression. Either the rebellion or the Master must win this contest in order to preserve a lasting peace. The Master would not stop once removed from power. He gave Citizens no choice. He must be the Master or he must be dead. The most heroic act a peaceful Citizen could take against the Master's repression was to respond with violence. Appeasement only encouraged more bloodshed.

The obvious site for the rematch was the Citadel. Geoff recognized the symbolism of the spot and so did the Master. Geoff did not expect a fair fight. He knew no quarter would be given. He doubted the Master would demonstrate honor in battle. Geoff's militia would be fighting wild beasts. The fighting would be savage and senseless. A genteel contest between well trained troops on the edge of town with victory going to the best dressed and best maneuvers would not suffice.

For this engagement Geoff needed to deliver an inspiring speech that did not mention retreat. The only words which adequately described the coming conflagration were bravery, sacrifice, and glory. Geoff was grateful Citizens had a taste of freedom before called upon to pay the ultimate price. He knew this battle would inspire acts of heroism for generations to come.

Once word was received that the Master was on the move Geoff summonsed his militia. Geoff let Soldiers from the old regime stay in the barracks and make their own decision to join his ranks. Only free will can overcome dogmatic training. A Soldier forced to fight one day might turn on you the next.

Geoff deployed his militia across from the Citadel. They took cover behind trees, porches, signposts, and anything that would deflect an arrow or sword. They knelt in a defensive position, making poor targets.

The Master force marched his troops through the Capitol to the steps of the Citadel, not giving pause for rest. He knew the thunder of a hard march intimidated the opposition. He let his most seasoned general speak for him. The general first addressed Soldiers in the Citadel.

"Rejoin the Master and reclaim your honor," was the first bargain.

"You will be paid handsomely," was an enticement Geoff could not counter.

"Come out before I have to come in," the general accelerated the deadline to decide.

A few Soldiers trickled out of the barracks, rejoining ranks with the Master's troops. Then the Master gave the order to massacre holdouts. His troops charged the barracks brandishing swords and clubs. Soldiers in the barracks did not have time to defend themselves. They didn't expect such immediate reprisal. Suffering was short but death was certain.

Geoff was shocked by the slaughter. He stepped out into the open from behind his protected vantage point, where his militia could see and hear him. His speech earlier that day called for personal sacrifice but now a new debt to all Mankind needed vindicating.

"You just witnessed savage animals brutalize fellow Citizens," Geoff testified to the Master's barbarism.

"Honor in battle does not tolerate such carnage," Geoff reminded his troops of the dignity in being a Soldier.

"The Master's troops do not fight to protect the Realm," Geoff condemned their motives.

"They fight for lust for power," Geoff argued against rehabilitation.

"They do not deserve headstones," Geoff dehumanized the criminals.

"The name of such a cruel Ruler should not appear in public," Geoff began to erase memory of the Master.

"Let your swords rewrite history," Geoff empowered his militia.

"Let the Master's blood cleanse his crimes," was the only ritual worthy of honoring slain Soldiers.

"Let God's speed deliver the righteous," Geoff released his militia with vengeance and permission.

Geoff's militia descended upon the Master slicing him into pieces too small to burry. Nothing stopped them, not arrow, club, or sword. They just kept slaying the Master's troops before them. The Master's troops ran in horror. Geoff's militia redoubled the Master's carnage. Once the bloodlust was released it could not be stopped. Geoff's militia impaled and beheaded the Master's troops all the way to the boarder. History was finally satisfied. None of the Master's troops lived to tell a different story.

Cleansed

The Realm had been cleansed. Bloodshed could be spared for another century until the stories of carnage no longer invoked horror. Blood dries then fades away. Blood soaked streets are washed clean by rain and commerce.

The Realm became remarkably easy to govern. No one had the stomach for more fighting. The Revolution lost its fervor. Even the counter-Revolution disappeared into futility. Life was dominated by apathy not political ambitions.

A Revolution was not a Revolution if there was no active rebellion. It is just the status quo. Complacent acquiescence to the mundane became the norm. Bloodshed cooled the revolutionary spirit as did slaughtering the Master in his Palace. Meritocracy was the consequence of murder. Vengeance needed no further proof of horror. The savage beast was put to rest.

Well placed messages attempted to revive the rebellion. The method of the message was its meaning. Slogans praising the Revolution appeared on banners placed about the Capitol. Criers for hire broadcast trivial accomplishments of the Revolution. Mimes in the park acted out themes that didn't need words like feeding the poor, driving Members from the Star Chamber, and slaying the Master. A Revolutionary troupe acted out more complex themes like creating the Oracle and forming the Tribunal. Few Citizens acknowledged their own history. They were not ready to synthesize a new thesis. The next scapegoat was needed to inspire their vigilance.

Uncommon Friendships

Geoff, Ann, and the Mathematician became good Friends. They shared a love for numbers. Geoff used numbers to make his machines. He could do calculations in his head that few other Citizens could match. For Geoff numbers were as real as the steel he pounded into shape.

Ann pioneered a new way of counting. She nested processes inside other processes ad infinitum. She devised a way to add, subtract, multiply, and divide any process an infinite series of times and still reach an answer. She knew how to remove infinity from a calculation in order to converge on a result.

The Mathematician was the strongest logician in the Realm. Reason dominated his thinking. All his ideas were in perfect balance with reality. One errant step in a long sequence of logic sorted itself out like planets settling into orbit. Each step reached its position by the weight of its persuasion and momentum of its conclusion. Thought was the essence of the Mathematician's being.

Each Friend contributed to the pursuits of the other. Geoff learned to package calculations into processes, starting and suspending one process until the result from another was ready to substitute into the chain to solve the calculation. Ann learned to make her new mathematics more practical, catering to tradesmen who needed tools to support their enterprise. The Mathematician focused on theory, realizing that knowledge for the sake of knowledge would eventually find an application, like a fantastic story about the future.

The three Friends held a special class to help formulate their knowledge. Attendees helped shape their ideas, refining the usable and discarding the superfluous. Knowledge flourished in the absence of government interdiction.

The Tribunal invited the Friends to make a presentation. Nothing was working to inspire Citizens to continue the Revolution. Maybe the Friends could teach the Tribunal how to motivate Citizens to reach their full potential.

"Why do Citizens attend your discussions," the Tribunal asked the Friends.

The Friends deferred to each other until one had the best answer.

"Because they get to design their own future," Ann explained.

"When duty is an obligation knowledge is uninspired," Ann conserved her words.

"Knowledge is the strongest force in nature," the Mathematician expanded his perspective.

"The other forces are hostage to its discovery," the Mathematician revealed.

"Knowledge is the most useful tool," Geoff added.

"Knowledge transforms itself into different applications as needed," Geoff spoke from experience.

"So how do we use knowledge to motivate Citizens to remain vigilant?" the Tribunal inquired.

"YOU DON'T," the Friends replied in a chorus.

"Freedom does that," Ann clarified.

Secret Session

The Tribunal convened a secret session. They had a crisis of confidence to resolve. Citizens grew apathetic toward duty. Left to govern themselves Citizens ignored the Tribunal. The rebellion replaced the Master with a Tribunal that failed to fill the vacuum. The Master created his own power whereas the Tribunal failed to.

The Tribunal appointed a panel to explore where power lay. The panel concluded that real power vests with enforcing laws. A written law is finished once enacted whereas enforcing law is never ending. Real power lay with the Court. A Court can enact all the laws it needs by enforcing any given law.

The panel's first step was to memorialize their appointments into permanent positions. They called themselves a "Commission" not a "Court". The word "Court" was still too repugnant to be used in public.

The Commission proclaimed to be above political entanglements. Commissioners denied all political affiliations. They emphasize their mandate was judicial not political. They denounced political ambitions.

The Commission rediscover the Master's paradox - "To Judge Is To Govern". It is the Court that commands obedience not the Tribunal. Governments come and go but Courts remain the same.

The Commission re-established Rules, a Code of Ethics, and licensed Members to practice their profession. They replaced the Oracle with the Commission's arbitrary and capricious judgements. Human prejudice was preferable to random injustice. While the Tribunal struggled to represent the will of the people the Commission represented its own will, not handicapped by democratic baggage. Some thought the Master's old Court was cruel by design but it was just the consequence of being a Court. Achieving Justice is as cruel as falling short. It is the cruelty you see not the injustice.

Seeking Justice is a non sequitur. It means too much to mean anything at all. Citizens are helpless to define Justice. Punishing crimes is not justice it is just revenge. Half a baby is not Justice because no one gets what they want. Resolving conflicts is not Justice because the truth is never really known, there's not enough time. Conflicts do not have a beginning or end, they simply continue.

Courts delve into Justice because Citizens don't dare to. Citizens are reluctant to judge whereas Courts rush to judgment. "Judge Not Want Not" is the received wisdom of the ages. Natural consequences are more effective of a judge than an uninformed jurist but little about the Court is natural.

Courts are an afterthought to government. Why create a body to misinterpret law? It is no accident that governments capitulate their power to judge. It is an impossible task. Why get involved in it? Enacting law is prestigious whereas passing judgment is prejudicial and petty.

Courts are like casinos allowing voyeurs to gamble. Citizens watch the Court like the crowd watches a hangman, one satisfies the other. Citizens tolerate Courts in hopes of witnessing something provocative.

Citizens are stuck with the Courts. The Court rises form the ashes and reinvents itself. The Court is like a distant cousin visiting the family. They show up and must be taken in. Revolution waists its time overthrowing the government. It is the Court that should be eliminated.

The Commission proclaimed an Edict to cure the Tribunal's crisis in confidence. The Commission announced it will act whenever the Tribunal remains silent. Laws not yet enacted are the Commission's prerogative to enforce. Power abhors a vacuum. The Commission must guide the Realm out of the abyss. Someone must be made accountable for Citizens' apathy. Persecution is too kind a word to limit the Commission's authority. When asked what will work to restore confidence Commissioners respond, "You'll know it when you see it".

The Realm was on thin ice, like a region waiting for invasion. Citizens felt guilty they were not better at governing. Their guilt was a weakness that could be exploited. Citizens wanted a perpetrator to be prosecuted so they could relax back into apathy. Sacrificing the innocent satisfied a perverse selfishness. Scapegoating is a ritual celebrating denial. Life is not fair and there are Courts to prove it. The more unsolvable the crime the more unjust the solution.

The Commission handed down an indictment identifying those responsible for inspiring apathy toward government. A sealed Writ of Attendance was served on the accused. It commanded their appearance before the Commission. No one else knew the identity of the accused. The Commission prepared for a public inquisition. Notices were posted about the Realm.

> Take Notice the Commission of the People's Court will conduct an inquiry into the ineffectiveness of the Tribunal," the Commission announced innocently enough.

The accused were incarcerated and held without bail. They were separated and did not know the other's identity. They went missing and no one knew their whereabouts. They were not presented with charges, provided counsel, or allowed to confess. They needed to serve as examples for all to scorn.

The Commission called itself into session. Opening remarks were short.

> "We assemble today to cure the Realm of apathy," was their grandiose pronouncement.

> "Apathy plagues the Tribunal with ineffectiveness," was their conclusion.

> "We have identified the cause and now propose a cure," the Commission drew attention to the accused.

"Present the accused," the Commission instructed the clerk.

The accused were led from their cells and presented to the Commission for arraignment. The crowd gasped. The accused were the finest Citizens in the Realm. If the accused were guilty then so was everyone else. Citizens recoiled in memory of the Revolution. They remembered sharing a bond with the accused and the rebellion. They fought along side the accused but are now paralyzed to defend them.

There stood Geoff, Ann and the Mathematician accused of sedition and surely to be found guilty. This was a sacrificial ritual not a judicial proceeding.

"We sentence you to hang until dead," the Commission ruled, jumping past allegation, evidence, argument, and rebuttal.

The outcome justified the complaint. Lesser charges would not satisfy the punishment. Death by hanging confirmed their guilt. Their crime was in being found guilty.

Geoff, Ann and the Mathematician stared into the crowd for support. They knew better though. The temperament of a crowd doesn't work that way. Crowds don't change their disposition in public. They are swayed in a direction and stay put. This crowd didn't want a hanging but they were going to watch anyway. They weren't going to judge. They were told that job belonged to the Commission.

The Commission sent the three Friends back to their cells to prepare for their execution. They were allowed to join company in their final days. No harm could come from their union when no defense could be presented against their charges.

Practicing to Die

Ann practiced back flips in her cell. Her Friends thought she had gone crazy. They were preparing for their execution while she worked out. To each their own the two men thought. They were satisfied their lives had been fulfilled. What an amazing evolution their lives had taken. From mere peasants to leaders of a Revolution. From outnumbered rebels to victorious Citizens. From cogs in the wheel to champions of change. Their only regret was that the change had not been lasting. Citizens slipped back into their bad habits of doing as told.

"What are you doing Ann?" Geoff asked, careful not to seem too worried considering their fate.

"We are to be hanged - Right?" Ann confronted the morose.

"Yes Ann. You know we are," Geoff was resigned to his fate.

"Well then, I'm practicing being hanged," Ann embraced the situation in full defiance.

The Mathematician studied her exercises, seeing more than just a back flip. Ann had a plan. She had torn her bedding into long strips, tying them into a rope. She tied the rope to the rafters and let it dangle to the floor like a hangman's noose.

"Ann, you can't take your own life," Geoff tried to stop

her from committing suicide.

"I can and will if it ever comes to that," Ann stuck up for her right to choose life or death.

Ann tied a noose in the end of the rope and slipped it over her head.

"No Ann," Geoff cried out, weeping in despair.

"See you on the other side," Ann bid farewell, hoping to land upright.

She bent at the knees and flipped backward, catching the rope between her legs while upside down in mid air, throwing a loop around her ankle. The rope snared tight around her leg, breaking her fall, never snapping her neck.

"Have you ever seen a man hanged," the Mathematician asked.

"My father," Ann revealed.

"Then you know your hands will be tied," the Mathematician was reluctant to inform.

"Did you see me use my hands?" Ann replied with confidence.

"No, And I didn't think it was an accident," the

Mathematician praised.

"I'm sorry I won't live to see you escape," Geoff couldn't stop crying and without a plan of his own.

"I will be the first to be hanged," Ann reassured Geoff.

"How does that help? I can't do a back flip," Geoff questioned her plan.

"Imagine the confusion on the gallows when I go through the trap door upside down," Ann began painting the picture.

Geoff paused and considered the image. He started to see opportunity for his escape as well.

A Farewell Visit

The Merchant had distanced himself from his three Friends after the rebellion. The Revolution had become too tumultuous and bad for business. The Merchant would return to his homeland if he still could. At least he would escape with Geoff's machine committed to memory.

But sentimentality got the better of his good judgment. He had to visit his Friends one more time. It would be his last chance to see them before they were hung.

The Merchant knew the rules of prison. Pay the guards, don't ask for permission to visit. A few coins would buy some time in private. But the Merchant wasn't taking any chances. He went in disguise. For all he knew there should be four prisoners, himself included.

At first the three Friends did not recognize the Merchant, until he spoke.

"Is there anything I can do?" the Merchant asked to comfort his friends.

"Attend our hanging," the Mathematician made a hard request.

"It will be my honor," the Merchant thought it was his duty to attend.

"Be prepared for some magic," Ann forewarned.

"That's not why they are hanging you," the Merchant tried to make light of the situation.

"Not this time," Ann agreed.

"Just be there," Geoff tried to protect his old partner from becoming implicated.

"You'll know what to do," the Mathematician assured.

The Merchant knew he should leave before he was told too much. He also knew his three Friends just confided in his trust to do what he could to help them escape. He felt he needed at least one clue what to look for.

"What will give your ruse away?" the Merchant asked for a warning.

"Acrobatics," Ann hinted.

The Execution

The Commission advertised the execution for weeks in advance. The entire Realm knew of the event. Opportunists sold tickets even though the spectacle was free. Citizens love a hanging like fools love a parade, it is going to happen anyway so you might as well watch.

On the fatal day Citizens packed the public square like bricks in a wall. There was no room to move closer to the gallows. Jugglers, clowns, and vendors entertained the crowd. The hanging brought the best out in Citizens. It was a chance to enjoy quality time with the family.

The Commissioners ascended the stairs to the top of the gallows. The three prisoners followed. There was only one trap door so the Commissioners had to decide who would be hung first. They offered the noose to the three Friends, letting them choose who won the honors. The Mathematician stepped forward offering his life, knowing his choice would be rejected. The Commissioners were not about to let one of the prisoners have their way. The Commissioners just smiled and shook their head no.

The choice was then between Geoff and Ann. Life had been reduced to a 50-50 chance. Geoff stepped forward, thinking the Commissioners would override his offer as well. But a familiar voice in the crowd cried out.

"Ladies first," the Merchant yelled and the crowd erupted

in laughter.

Commissioners had not anticipated Citizens bonding over such a macabre show. They looked at each other for agreement and decided Ann should go first.

The designated Commissioner stepped forward to the front of the gallows to read the indictment. The crowd paid no attention. They didn't appreciate the formalities. It had been years since the Master staged a hanging and they were growing impatient.

The hangman slung the noose over Ann's neck. He tied her hands behind her back. He seized her arm and muscled her over the trap door, enraging Geoff. Geoff rushed the hangman who backhanded Geoff, knocking him off his feet. The Commissioners quickly intervened in the skirmish not wanting to start a riot. You could hang an innocent Citizen but you could not abuse them.

The crowd was getting an eye full but they did not notice Ann inching her way past the edge of the trap door, balancing on the precipice of death. Her toes clinched the edge of the platform just past trap door like a bird clinches a branch, holding on for dear life. The Commissioners looked back and forth and then nodded to the hangman.

Ann watched the hangman out of the corner of her eye, ready to spring into a back flip the instant he released the door. He paused for a instant, stealing the moment for his own show, wanting the crowd to reach anxious expectation. The crowd leaned forward, reaching to meet the snap of Ann's neck. Then the hangman threw the lever.

"O-H-H!" the crowd exhaled, making the sound of freefall- before the crush of the rope snapped Ann's neck.

But there was no freefall. There was no snap. There was just Ann seeming to hover weightless over the hole in the gallows made by the release of the trap door.

Then she sprung into air, flipping backward, catching the rope with her foot on the way up. At the top of her assent she was looking downward centering herself on the trap door. She accelerated past the hangman and Commissioners who were caught in a fog trying to figure out what was happening. She felt the rope snap tight around her leg slowing her descent. At the bottom of the rope she wiggled out of the noose and dropped to the ground. She hid behind the apron around the gallows meant to shield the crowd from witnessing her retching body.

The hangman ventured over the hole opened by the trap door, leaning far forward to inspect Ann's condition. Geoff and the Mathematician charged the hangman knocking him through the hole. They landed in a pile at Ann's feet. She wrestle the hangman's knife away that he intended to cut her down with after she stopped breathing.

The crowd rushed the gallows to look for the missing corpse. Ann's death defying leap turned the hanging into a magic show. The push of the crowd caused a stampede. The Merchant circled around back of the gallows to lead his Friends away to safety. He brought costumes to disguise their notoriety. They merged into the chaos and slipped out of sight without being apprehended.

The Mathematician had no theory for explaining the improbability of their survival. Geoff realized he was being protected by a higher force - Ann. Ann was busy planning her next miracle. The Merchant had just saved the Realm from further demise.

Revelation

The Merchant returned to his homeland where culture outlived political turmoil. The three Friends were already home, where they were born and raised. They had no place else to go. They had a formidable task ahead - to survive. They had to be realistic. They failed to anticipate the failure of the Tribunal and re-emergence of the Court. It was as if the Court had its own life despite their intentions. Whatever the rebellion did to extinguish the Court failed to douse the flame. They needed to treat the Court as though it housed an insidious predator. The Star Chamber clearly harbored an evil spirit and they failed to fully appreciate the mythology.

Ordinary Citizens were not the enemy. It was apparent they would do as told. The enemy was the spirit residing in the Star Chamber. The Friends needed to change their methods from leading a rebellion to performing an exorcism. They had been too impressed with their success rewriting history to recognize superior forces. Evil can not be driven from the Court unless it is confronted on its own terms.

It is best to challenge evil in teams of three. Evil itself often appears in apparitions of three. Darkness in the Star Chamber appeared as Master, Member, and Money Lender. Judge, Clerk, and Marshal make another triplet. This was tricky stuff. Reason must surrender to ritual.

The Mathematician's belief in evil was not based on knowledge. He could not hear, see, or touch evil but presumed its existed. Nothing else explained Citizens' inability to manage their own destiny. Their future was secure until the Court sprang back to life.

The Mathematician was not preoccupied with proof. He did not limit possibilities by rigid framework. His bricks were set in mud not mortar. For a theory to work it only had to explain the outcome. Cause was rarely knowable. Outcomes were certain whereas cause was illusive. Cause depends on time moving forward whereas evil has no such constraint.

The Mathematician must resort to allies in a place no one else thought to look.

A Trip to the Monastery

Citizens of the Realm did not go to Church. The Master forbid it when he was alive. He didn't need the competition. Religion was practiced in the Monastery, not a Church. Monks sequestered in worshiped didn't threaten the Master. The Master thought Monks worshiping in isolation was a good lesson for Citizens. If Citizens openly worship another Master he banished them into seclusion.

The Mathematician suspected Monks possessed special powers unknown to ordinary Citizens. Why else would they worship all day and night unless there was a personal reward.

Ann knew more than most about Monks. Her father had studied at the Monastery before he was hung for spreading religion throughout the Realm. As a child she observed her father meditate in prayer and use candles, incense, and purified water in rituals. He chanted in a rhythmic melody, breathing words into the air to give them power. She mimicked his rituals in private and discovered their effect. Her insight into mathematics flowed from these sessions. The Monks taught her father to commune with God. Without her own mentor Ann learned to commune with the Universe.

The Mathematician told Ann he suspected Monks might have special powers.

"I'm going to the Monastery. Do you want to come," the Mathematician invited.

"Be careful," Ann warned, well aware of the risks.

"What is it?" Geoff interjected, sensing trouble.

"Once you enter their world compromise is not an option," Ann knew the conditions of true power.

"I did not know you were a believer?" the Mathematician said as a question.

"More like a seer," Ann clarified, "I believe what I have seen".

The Mathematician didn't doubt her one bit. He learned not to doubt anything about Ann. She seemed to have a direct channel on truth.

The three Friends departed for the Monastery. There were no roads into or out of the area. There was not even a foot path to guide the way. No one ever went there, or left. Ann was guided by a memory buried deep in her childhood. She remembered how shadows fell, dirt smelled, and the breeze felt. The way to the Monastery came back like heirlooms stored for safe keeping. She looked up and they were at the Monastery steps.

The front door to the Monastery was always ajar. Visitors didn't need permission to enter. Everyone was welcome. An old frail Monk greeted the three Friends at the threshold. Ann felt the rush of bittersweet sorrow fill her eyes with tears. There stood her father's mentor as if waiting all these years for her to return. They joined hands when words would not do. They hugged in a long embrace. He kissed her on the forehead, wiping the tears from her cheeks.

"Please meet my Friends," Ann introduced Geoff and the Mathematician to the Monk.

"We've been waiting for you," the Monk wanted them to feel connected and at home.

"And evidently I've been waiting for you," the Mathematician recognized their destiny.

"Let's go into the garden," the Monk directed, knowing it would be a long talk.

"And this young man, not just a friend?" the Monk asked of Geoff.

"Once a friend, now a servant," Geoff began to recognize his fate.

"Worship begins than with service to others," the Monk blessed their union.

Ann reached out for Geoff's hand. She had never shown a gesture of affection toward him before. He had waited patiently for their friendship to grow past tolerance and fraternal sharing into a bond no mortal could break.

"Here is what I know," the Monk began.

"The Master is dead but his ghost haunts the Court and Tribunal. Citizens are apathetic because free will alone is not the source of power. Free will is just the beginning of the story. It is only a day in a year. Citizens did not choose the rebellion, it was thrust upon them. Changing the outcome requires changing what's inside. The material world is a distraction. Citizens must work to see past physical obstructions and concentrate on knowing their own mind. In focusing on focusing a certain resonance is reached where minds join in a harmonic pulse, like hearts beating together in a race. Nothing good happens without exercise. These are not secrets, they are only tools."

"So we should stage mass exercises doing what?" the Mathematician didn't think he quite understood.

"Singing, chanting, praying, meditating," the Monk was quick to answer.

"What are the words to the songs?" the Mathematician sought deeper insight.

"It doesn't matter at first," the Monk assured.

"All roads lead to the center. The words are not the destination," the Monk tried to explain.

"Do you have words you know will work," the Mathematician wanted more proof.

"I have some favorites, like nursery rhymes," the Monk seemed to joke, willing to keep the message shrouded in mystery.

"I fear what will happen when we expose themes concealed in mythology," the Mathematician was reluctant to explore the topic.

"The fear comes from the concealment not from the exposure," the Monk knew from experience.

"Try this - ," the Monk offered.

"There is a game we play at the Monastery that involves a ball and a drum," the Monk began to explain a way into the mind.

"We form a circle and toss the ball around and around. The drummer tries to keep beat with us. He speeds up the tempo and so do we. Then someone breaks with the pattern and passes the ball across the circle. That speeds up until the ball is in the air more than not. We once played this game all day. The ball seemed to levitate without our touch. Our catches and throws became the same. Our breathing became one."

"Do you know where the ball lands," the Monk proposes.

"In the center," to confirm that the inside controls the outside.

The Mathematician pinched his chin to ponder the possibilities. Could it be that belief is more powerful than knowledge. He must put personal power to a test.

The Procession

Ann, Geoff, and the Mathematician donned hooded robes worn by the Monks. They all filed into the Capitol in a block long procession. Citizens had only heard of the Monks and followed them in curiosity. The procession went to the public square where the three Friends were almost hanged. The gallows was still erected, waiting for their recapture. The Monks formed a circle around the gallows. The drummer went to the top of the platform to start the rhythm. They began passing their ball, only it resembled a severed head. It had the look of a grotesque face separated from its body. Citizens were captivated by the display, wondering if they had missed a hanging. The Monks began a low vibrating chant, like a chorus of bullfrogs croaking in the summer marsh. One at a time the Monks climbed the stairs to the top of the gallows and jumped through the open trap door. Once on the ground the Monks reassembled in front of the gallows and took a bow.

The crowd did not know what they were witnessing. Was it an act, a game, or were the Monks just crazy?

The Monks began the bullfrog chant again and started passing the ball. Citizens felt more comfortable and joined in. The chant changed to a song.

"Playing seems wrong when there's work to do,"

"But life passes by if left to you,"

"Take time to play before,"

"The hours are gone and no more."

The ball dropped to the ground. Citizens were caught in a spell. They all had the same dumbfounded look and stood in the same slouched stance. The Monks sang another song, this one rigged to sneak into the dream.

"Play is work and song is good,"

"Judging others is misunderstood,"

"Courts do not have the right to rule,"

"Rights come from another world."

The Monks quietly separated from the crowd, disappearing back to the Monastery. One by one Citizens awoke from the spell, humming the harmonic cadence of the bullfrog song.

"Rights come from another world," they were sure of it.

The story of their abduction circulated throughout the Realm. Citizens could not account for time spent in the public square that day. The last thing they remembered were Monks jumping through the trap door. And everyone was humming "Rights come from another world" but no one knew where the song came from.

The slogan "Rights come from another world" appeared on banners flown in the public square. The slogan was painted on walls. It appeared as an argument in Court. It was used as a defense against cruel and unusual punishment, like death by hanging without a trial. The Commission had to put a stop to it.

The Commission issued another Edict.

"Citizens who write, speak, or reference the obscenity 'Rights come from another world' will be sentenced to death", the proclamation warned.

Citizens tried to get the offensive rhyme out of their mind. But the Monks had another song to teach Citizens to replace the first song. Monks dressed in ordinary clothing and filtered back into the Capitol. They assembled on the Courthouse steps in a chorus of two dozen. They began humming the bullfrog song, lulling Citizens into a mid day slumber.

"This world comes with other rights," the Monks changed the lyrics.

"Ten or more and worth the fight," they got down to it.

"It is not the Master, Man, or Government," the Monks readied the crowd.

"Who joins you in a covenant,"

"These rights can not be taken,"

"If you will fight and awaken."

Each Monk dropped a torn piece off the same drawing, as proof of their appearance. Then they disappeared as before. The pieces of the drawing resembled a puzzle. Citizens took time to put the picture back together. The torn edges helped match the pieces in the right order.

It was clear what the picture looked like, just not what it meant. There were no words, only symbols. A horizontal line with a triangle emanating from below the midpoint was inscribed within a circle.

Without all the tears it looked like .

Citizens guessed its meaning.

"It is the Master's scales seen through the keyhole looking into the Star Chamber," one visionary was sure.

"Scales in the Star Chamber" seemed to stick.

"Rights come from another world,"

"This world comes with other rights,"

"Scales in the Star Chamber are worth the fight."

This story has been told from time immemorial. Pagan worshipers traced the origin of our rights to the bullfrog song. Another legend holds that rights descended to Earth through a trap door from heaven, along with the King. A group of wise Founders envisioned that rights were the unalienable birthright of Mankind. Geoff and Ann spread word that rights were first celebrated by singing Monks who had no political ambitions. Regardless where rights come from it is certain they do not come from the court or government.

Rumors of Rumors

Rumors of the Assassin resurfaced. Citizens believed the Assassin rescued Geoff, Ann, and the Mathematician from hanging. Citizens also thought the Assassin protected Monks when they fought to bring rights to the Realm. Citizens expected the Assassin would move against the Commission.

The Mathematician assumed the real assassins were still active. He knew the rumored Assassin was a ghost but the real assassins had struck before. The Mathematician was determined to find them.

The Mathematician needed to avoid discovery. He would be hanged if caught again. He was safe in the Monastery but finding the real assassins required taking risks.

The power of assumption was the Mathematician's most formidable weapon. He assumed the real assassins existed and were avoiding discovery like he was. The Mathematician assumed the real assassins would strike the Commission because it needed to be done. The Mathematician's task was to give the real assassins cover by way of rumor in order to help them operate.

Thanother sighting of the ghost Assassin. The Mathematician enlisted Geoff's help to fabricate convincing evidence the Assassin still operated freely. Geoff and the Mathematician entered the Capitol at night to spread posters advertising a bounty on Commissioners. The poster promised the

Assassin would pay for proof of a Commissioner's death. An arrow through the heart brought the highest reward, a severed head brought a lesser amount. Report of a Commissioner's disappearance brought an even smaller reward.

The Mathematician let the offer of reward do its work. Commissioners stopped conducting trials. They cleared their calendar so as not to be assessable. Members could not get their cases settled or get paid by their clients. The rival Tribunal started enacting laws of its own in the Commission's absence. A new office of the Tribunal had to be created to hear and settle disputes. The vacant Commission was losing its influence.

The Commissioners needed protection. But the standing militia only protected the Tribunal not the Commission. Commissioners needed to hire their own guards but they had no funds for such luxuries. Their only option was to charge a fee for their decisions. They must issue a new Edict that Citizens must pay to appear before them - retroactively.

Commissioners wanted to hire guards who had no prior allegiances in the Realm. Loyalty could be purchased if affiliations were uncomplicated. Guards must be virtually anonymous, native born, and unbeholden to others.

The Mathematician convinced Monks to dress as Citizens and apply for the job. The Mathematician thought lesser known Monks posing as ordinary Citizens would be preferable to Commissioners over better known Citizens with higher rank and status. Monks who no one knew and who had no associations to complicate their employment were ideal candidates except they could not prove their citizenship. They were too unknown. But that was the Mathematician's intent - to frustrate Commissioners in their search for protection. A month went by without Commissioners finding guards they could trust. The Monk's ruse created the perfect opportunity for the real assassins to apply instead.

The real assassins could not resist the chance to infiltrate the Commission. They had all the qualifications for the job of protector. They were locals, unimplicated by commitments, and relatively unknown. One had served in the army but without distinction. Another was a jack of all trades but master of none. And the third appeared to be a nobody.

The real assassins were not political or impressed by power. They wanted the job of body guard because they hated bullies. The real assassins despised the Master and Commissioners because these leaders victimized innocent Citizens. In a more civil Realm the real assassins might have remained as apathetic as other Citizens. But in that more civil Realm bullies would have been punished before they rose to power. In that more civil Realm bullies would have been ridiculed instead of rewarded. A righteous calling provoked the real assassins to act out of principle, not out of lesson, obedience, or fame.

The Mathematician knew all the Monks who were rejected by Commissioners so he assumed the real assassins were the last to apply. After the real assassins met with Commissioners the

Mathematician thought it was safe to contact them but neither side could reveal their true identity to the other. The Mathematician wrapped fifty coins in a wanted poster and dispatched a massager to deliver the package to the real assassins. The real assassins were forced to decide if the money was a ploy by Commissioners or a contribution from the rebellion.

The real assassins decided the money must be a test of loyalty devised by Commissioners. The Mathematician anticipated as much. He hoped the real assassins would not be so easily enticed by money from an unknown benefactor. The real assassins reported the bribe to their future employer. Commissioners were now certain they had the right candidates for the job. The Mathematician's strategy conducted in the dark was paying off.

The first task Commissioners assigned the real assassins was to collect fees for Commissioners' prior decisions. The real assassins realized they were raising revenue to pay their own wages. They had no interest in subjecting Citizens to more despair but committing to the Commissioners gave the real assassins cover for their next plan.

It was time for the Mathematician to pose as the ghost Assassin and give real life to the rumor. The Mathematician planned to kidnap a Commissioner and arrange for the reward to be paid by the Assassin. The Monastery was the perfect sanctuary to hide the hostage. No one would venture into the forest to look for an official everyone despised.

The Mathematician filed a false complaint to get on the Commission's docket. He requested a meeting with Commissioners to discuss a potential settlement. Before the meeting the Mathematician sent the most corrupt Commissioner an advanced payment and requested a separate meeting. Monks were ready to intercept the Commissioner and usher him away. These were easy maneuvers in a Realm new to intrigue. No one had ever thought to double cross the Master because a foiled attempt would have been fatal.

Once the Commissioner went missing the reward for his disappearance was due. But who would pay it? Better yet who would claim it?

The Monks donated another hefty sum to pay the reward. They sent the money to the real assassins once again. Only this time the real assassins kept the reward, realizing it was futile to surrender it to Commissioners. This was no longer a test, it was an instruction.

The real assassins knew there was only one other group as stealthy as them. The real assassins knew Geoff and the Mathematician must be trying to make contact. The real assassins no longer feared surveillance by Commissioners. It must be Geoff and the mathematician who were watching. Each group had to assume the other was conducting the same mission.

The Mathematician planned for the abduction of the remaining two Commissioners. He sent message to the real assassins when and where the exchange should happen. The real assassins cooperated by escorting Commissioners out of the Capitol supposedly for their own safety. On the road to the hiding place a band of Monks surrounded the Commissioners. Geoff and the Mathematician sprung from the center of the raiding party to intercept the real assassins. Geoff ordered the real assassins to drop their weapons. The Monks took quick custody of the Commissioners and disappeared into the forest. Geoff told the real assassins to return to the Capitol to report the ambush. The rumored Assassin had struck again.

Citizens took notice that apathy had consequences. If Citizens would not act then bullies and assassins would. If the rebellion did not remain vigilant the counter-Revolution would. If the Tribunal did not govern the Court would. If legitimate Rulers did not maintain power tyrannical despots would. When power is taken virtue is the first casualty. In the end it was the rumored Assassin who protected the rights of Citizens.